To Paul,

Pandora's

Socks

Gary Renison

Gary Renison.

ISBN 978-1-4716-3408-6

Cover Artwork: Kip Crookes

For

Jessica & Joe

Simon & Hannah

1

Pandora Johnson's mum was having a baby. She was now so huge that she wobbled unsteadily wherever she went like a jelly that needed more time to set. And because her mum was having a baby, and because it would be arriving soon, Pandora's family was moving in a few days time to a different house.

As their new house was only up the street and round the first corner on the left, it wasn't as if they were going very far. Their move could hardly be called a great adventure. Pandora wouldn't even have to change schools, and her dad could still catch the bus to work from the same stop as he did now.

But their new house was bigger. Most importantly, it had a third bedroom. There would be one for Pandora (which she was going to have painted yellow, whatever her dad said), another for her parents (including an ensuite with a shower that dripped) and a third (the smallest, naturally) for the new baby.

And because Pandora's mum was having a baby and the family was moving house, Pandora's mum and dad needed extra furniture, including some different bedroom furniture for Pandora. She was going to donate the bed, chest of drawers and wardrobe she used at the moment to the baby. Pandora didn't mind giving them away one little bit. They were far too small. Worse, the chest of drawers was covered with embarrassingly bad pictures of farm animals painted by her dad with far more enthusiasm than talent. The furniture had been too babyish for years - something about which she had complained many times. Pandora was determined her new bedroom furniture was going be much more grown up, without a weird orangey pig or blue-green cow in sight.

Except that it wasn't actually going to be new. Apart for the bed, that is. Pandora's mum was worried about fleas and bugs; hence the new bed. But she clearly wasn't worried about woodworm, because the rest of the furniture was to be second hand. Pandora and her dad were going to buy the wardrobe and chest of drawers on Saturday from Mr. Brewster's Furniture Emporium - a rather posh name, grumbled Pandora continuously, for what was only after all a second hand shop - as they didn't have much money, with the baby coming and the move.

Which brings us rather neatly to the point of this story. It's all to do with the second hand chest of drawers Pandora's dad bought for Pandora's new bedroom because they were moving house as her mum was having a baby.

Of course, if they had gone to IDEA, like Lucy's mum and dad did when Lucy had a new bedroom, then none of it would have happened. At least, it would not have happened to Pandora.

But they didn't go to IDEA. They went to Mr. Brewster's Furniture Emporium.

And so it did.

2

It was early Saturday morning. Pandora was lying in her bed (soon to be the baby's) looking around her bedroom (soon to be someone else's) thinking about her new bedroom (which most definitely had to be yellow).

The previous night Pandora's dad had ordered her new bed on the Internet. It was the first time he had ever bought anything using a computer. He had been drinking a second glass of beer at the time. He had also been singing. Pandora wasn't at all sure her dad had clicked on the correct part of the screen, not just because he is useless at computers - which he is - but because of the beer. She had more than a sneaking suspicion he had ordered a beanbag, which was the one before bed on the list. They'd soon find out. The bed (or beanbag) was due to be waiting for them at their new house on Wednesday, the day of their move.

Pandora slid slowly out of bed and took her favourite yellow t-shirt and jeans from the little chair in the corner of her room, their resting place from the day before. Pandora dressed thoughtfully. To be honest, she felt very mixed about going shopping with her dad. Part of her was really happy, as she loved spending time with him and it was a real treat for it to be just the two of them. But another part was a sort of mixture of cross and sad. Pandora didn't very much want furniture that someone else had used before. A yellow bedroom needed new furniture.

Her mum was already in the kitchen standing by the sink when Pandora walked in. She wasn't doing anything. Being pregnant meant she got out of lots of jobs. She was listening to the radio and drinking a mug of steaming tea. She still had on her nightie and dressing gown. Both had given up trying to fit her weeks before, and looked as strained and tired as Pandora's mum sometimes did.

"Good morning, Pandora," said her mum, holding the mug to her chin and smiling through the wispy mist. "Are we crisping or crunching today?"

"Crunching," replied Pandora, picking up a spoon and taking her seat at the kitchen table. "I'm starving."

Pandora's mum poured a pile of Crunchy Cornflakes into one of the big blue bowls that Auntie Emily had given her mum and dad last Christmas. Pandora added milk from the carton and began to munch happily.

"Did Charlie move much in the night?" asked Pandora after a couple of mouthfuls. Charlie was the name her mum and dad had already given the baby. It suited boys and girls equally as well and they didn't know what their baby was yet.

"Move!" exclaimed her mum, raising her eyes to the ceiling in an exasperated sort of way. "It was like trying to sleep with two five-a-side teams using my insides as a football pitch! At one point I felt like keeping score. I hardly closed my eyes, Pandora. When you and Dad have gone out I'm going back to bed. Being pregnant is so tiring."

"Where is Dad?" inquired Pandora, accidentally dribbling milk down her chin as she spoke and wiping it with the back of her hand. "Has he had his breakfast?"

"He's already eaten," replied her mum. "He's outside with Mr. Mower. Mr. Mower has said we can borrow his van to bring back your furniture. As it is Saturday he doesn't need it for work, and it's much bigger than our car, even with the back seat down. They're emptying it out as much as they can."

Pandora liked Mr. Mower. He was a plumber. He lived in the last house of their terrace with his wife and a lively white Scottie dog called Tam. Mr. Mower said the name was short for Tam O'Shanter, which he explained was a sort of bobble hat made of tartan, though Pandora didn't understand why a hat should have to have a name like that. Mr. Mower whistled very loudly whenever he was getting into or out of his van. This always made Tam bark and wag his tail frantically as he stood on the sofa by the living room window. The whistling and barking was a special sort of greeting between them, and only ever happened when Mr. Mower was whistling by the van. As she swallowed the last mouthful of her cereal Pandora's dad came in. He was extremely sweaty and had grubby hands. He smiled and kissed Pandora on the cheek.

"Are you ready, Pandora?" he asked, as he plunged his hands into the washing up bowl. "Your carriage awaits you, my lady."

"I just need to clean my teeth and brush my hair," said Pandora. She jumped off her chair and gave the bowl and spoon to her mum, who plopped them in the water next to her dad's hands.

"Well, be quick," called out her dad. He dried himself on a tea towel before making his way back outside. "I want to beat the traffic."

"I won't be long," replied Pandora. She rushed upstairs to the bathroom and got herself ready.

Within minutes she was sitting next to her dad in the front seat of Mr. Mower's van. It smelt strongly of fish and chips, and had lots of empty chocolate wrappers lined up along the dusty dashboard. The van made strange noises as Pandora's dad started the engine, as if it wasn't at all sure about making a journey on its day off. But at least it had plenty of room.

"Soon be there," said Pandora's dad cheerily as they pulled away and joined the thin trickle of traffic making its way early into town. "At least we won't need to worry about parking at this time of the day. Mr. Brewster has plenty of spaces round the back."

Pandora sat quietly in the worn out passenger seat as the van chugged along. She wondered what Mr. Brewster's Furniture Emporium would be like. Mum said there would be lots of choice, and that the furniture Mr. Brewster sold was in good condition, even if it some of it was very old. She said, too, that Dad could always give what they bought a good clean and polish, or even a fresh lick of paint.

As they turned into the High Street they passed a shiny new lorry with the words 'IDEA' written proudly in big blue and black letters on the side. Two men were loading furniture into the back. It looked crisp and clean and was wrapped tightly in cellophane. Another man was getting ready to make the deliveries. Suddenly, Pandora wished her mum wasn't having a baby, and that she was still at work so they had lots of money to buy whatever they wanted. Lucy didn't have any brothers or sisters. Instead, she had piano lessons and was learning to ride a pony. And she had got her chest of drawers delivered in a lorry like that.

Pandora was still feeling cross as the van pulled off the High Street and snaked its way past the butchers into the car park behind Mr. Brewster's Furniture Emporium. Dad turned off the engine, which sounded mightily relieved.

"Here we are, Pandora," said Dad as he undid his seatbelt. "Let's go and see what we can find for your new bedroom, shall we?"

3

To be honest, the Emporium was not at all what Pandora had expected. She had imagined a place piled high with grubby tables and broken chairs, the shabby sort of things people couldn't bring themselves to give to a jumble sale in case they were not sold and came back at the end of the day.

But the Emporium wasn't like that in the slightest. As they entered the back doors of the store and weaved their way towards the front desk Pandora's eyes opened wider and wider in amazement. The Emporium was packed floor to ceiling with the sort of furniture that invited you to stretch out your hand and touch it. Everything gleamed and smelt wonderfully of fresh polish. The grain in the different woods seemed darker and richer than any Pandora had ever seen before. It was as if, being older, the furniture had stopped being shy and could at last enjoy its beauty. Pandora began to feel excited about what she might find.

A young woman at the front desk pointed to a plan on the wall. It showed how Mr. Brewster arranged the furniture. It was neatly displayed in several different rooms. Bedroom and bathroom furniture was upstairs, as in a house. The rest was spread throughout the ground floor.

Dad thanked the girl and gripped Pandora by the hand. He led her past a row of military looking grandfather clocks, all standing stiffly to attention, and up the stairs to where the wardrobes and chests of drawers were on display.

At the top of the stairs they found Mr. Brewster. He had his back to them. He was talking with an elderly gentleman. On the floor between them was an old blanket box. The box had a hinged lid, which was opened. It glistened, inside and out. Mr. Brewster was agreeing a date and time for the blanket box to be delivered.

Pandora and Dad waited patiently until Mr. Brewster had finished dealing with the man. He turned next to serve them.

Pandora had never met anyone like Mr. Brewster before. She took to him instantly. He was a tall, thin man, with hardly any hair on his head, but with huge tufts of it, like the tops of carrots, sprouting out of his ears. It looked like he was letting off steam. For a moment, Pandora found it hard not to giggle. He was wearing a brown overcoat, immaculately pressed trousers and shiny black shoes. Under his overcoat he wore a checked shirt and a smart red tie. On his top lip rested a thin grey moustache, like a caterpillar that had found a convenient place to pass the time of day. His eyes sparkled like twinkly Christmas tree lights. Mr. Brewster looked at Pandora and winked kindly, before giving his full attention to Pandora's Dad.

"How can I help you, sir?" asked Mr. Brewster politely. His voice sounded as if it had been soaked in honey.

"We are moving house on Wednesday," explained Pandora's Dad. "We need a wardrobe and chest of drawers for Pandora's new bedroom. Have you anything suitable?"

"Ones that go with yellow," added Pandora hopefully.

"Follow me," said Mr. Brewster, beaming brightly. "I think I might have just the thing."

He led them along a corridor. The wall was covered with old pictures of meadows and streams. On various cabinets were glass cages full of stuffed animals and birds. They went through a door at the end. Inside the light and airy room a number of matching pairs of wardrobes and chests of drawers nestled neatly together.

"I am sure you will find something here for the young lady," said Mr. Brewster, his eyes twinkling. "Please feel free to touch anything. We positively encourage it here. Wood is rather like a cat, you know. It purrs contentedly when it is stroked. I will be back shortly to see how you are getting on."

With a polite nod Mr. Brewster went out of the room, leaving Pandora and her dad on their own.

"This place is great," whispered Pandora in a low voice when she was sure they were alone. "It's not at all like I thought it was going to be. How old do you think Mr. Brewster is?"

"Not even half as old as some of his furniture," said Dad smiling. "Have a good look around, Pandora. Tell me if there is anything you like."

It took no time at all for Pandora to decide. As they had entered the room a wardrobe and chest of drawers had instantly caught her eye. They had turned almost golden with age. What's more, they were set next to a window hung with yellow curtains. The curtains were exactly the same shade of yellow Pandora wanted in her new bedroom. It seemed as if the furniture had been made to go with yellow curtains.

Her heart began to pound with anticipation. Pandora almost ran over to examine them in more detail.

The wardrobe was tall and proud. It had two doors that opened outwards from the centre. Pandora pulled them open wide. The doors creaked in a chatty sort of way as they swung on their huge brass hinges, as if they were cheerily greeting the opener. For a moment Pandora thought of Lucy's wardrobe. It was silent when the doors opened. It was as if her wardrobe had nothing interesting to say.

Each door had a loopy brass handle in the shape of a long teardrop. Inside was a shiny brass bar that went all the way across from side to side. There was plenty of room for Pandora to hang all her clothes from this. At the base of the wardrobe were two drawers, one under each door. In them small pieces of clothing could be stored comfortably.

The chest of drawers was shorter and fatter. It had two thin drawers at the top that met respectfully in the middle, and three further drawers underneath that went all the way across. The bottom three drawers were huge and deep, and would hold masses of clothes and toys. They slid open noiselessly. The two top drawers had brass keyholes in the centre. Pandora tried to open them, but they were locked. She presumed Mr. Brewster had the key downstairs at the front desk. Pandora decided she would keep her precious things in there, like her diary, so Charlie would never be able to get them.

Pandora turned around excitedly. At that moment she wanted these two pieces of furniture more than anything else. Much more than anything that could be bought from any department store.

"Dad, can I have these?" pleaded Pandora. "They will look wonderful in my new bedroom. Look how they match the curtains!"

"I'll go and find Mr. Brewster," replied her dad, "and we'll see how much they cost. Then we'll decide. You stay here while I go and see where he is."

Dad went out of the room. Pandora turned back to the furniture. She remembered that Mr. Brewster had said his furniture liked to be stroked. Tenderly Pandora rubbed her hands along the top of the chest of drawers, imagining the wood purring beneath her touch. Then she began silently tracing the lines and whirls in the grain. It felt like she was carving her name into the wood itself.

It was as her finger was tracing a whirl shaped like the neck of a particularly graceful swan, that Pandora heard a noise. It was muffled and unclear, and sounded just like it does when people are sharing a secret. Pandora turned around abruptly. But there was no one else in the room. Dad had not yet returned with Mr. Brewster and no one else had entered. She went out into the corridor. No one was there, either. Pandora shrugged her shoulders. She presumed someone downstairs must have made the sound, probably other customers discussing a piece of furniture on the floor below. She returned to the room and carried on outlining the whirls with her finger.

After a few moments the noise came again. Pandora stopped tracing immediately. At the same time she yanked her hand away from the chest of drawers sharply, like she was suddenly afraid of being bitten. For in that moment Pandora thought she knew exactly where the noise was coming from. Incredible as it seemed, it sounded to Pandora like the noise was coming from *inside* the chest of drawers!

Pandora's immediate reaction was to run and fetch her dad and Mr. Brewster. She darted across the room to the doorway. Then she stopped abruptly. What if she was wrong? What if the sound was just the hushed echo of other people's voices? What if she was imagining the sound? She would look very stupid if she were making a fuss over nothing. Pandora decided to make certain before she did anything more.

She crept back across the room as quietly as she could. By walking on tip toes and taking huge strides Pandora managed to reach the chest of drawers without as much as a squeak from the floorboards to give away her stealthy return. Nervously she lifted her thick, auburn hair away from her ear. She knelt against the side of the chest of drawers and placed her ear as close to the wood as she dare. Holding her breath, Pandora listened hard.

In no time at all she heard it again. The noise sounded even louder to her now finely tuned ears. This time there could be no doubt. The sound was definitely coming from inside the chest of drawers. Furthermore, it seemed to be coming from deep within one of the two locked drawers!

Pandora pulled her head away, but slowly. Strangely, no longer did she feel as if all she wanted to do was run away and get help. Her fear was still present in the rapid beating of her heart, but another and altogether stronger sensation was overtaking her initial alarm. Pandora was becoming more curious than anything else. She suddenly wanted to know *what* was making the sound, and to find out for herself. Of course, Pandora knew what was in there could be very dangerous. After all, for some reason it had found its way into a locked drawer, one that must have been secured from the outside, probably deliberately. There were very good reasons, therefore, for telling her dad and Mr. Brewster all about the noise. But the temptation not to say anything was immense – and oddly exciting. Pandora began furiously to think over what she should do.

After a second or two she heard her dad and Mr. Brewster returning along the corridor. Their footsteps and voices quickly grew louder. In the moments before they reached the door Pandora made her decision. She resolved there and then to say absolutely nothing to anyone at this stage, except to Lucy, of course. She and Lucy would unlock the drawers together.

Pandora jumped to her feet and shook her hair back into place. She smiled as the men walked into the room and acted as if nothing had happened.

"Your father and I have agreed a price for the furniture," announced Mr. Brewster.

Pandora squealed with delight and threw her arms around her dad.

"However, there is something you need to know about the chest of drawers before you agree to have it. Something that might be of some concern to you." Mr. Brewster coughed apologetically and his face became grave.

Pandora's smile faded. Her heart sank. She let go of her dad. Mr. Brewster sounded serious. What if he already knew about the noise? Worse, what if he knew what was making it, and the whole thing turned out to be not very exciting after all? As Mr. Brewster continued, however, it became clear he knew nothing whatsoever about the secret hidden in the drawer.

"Unfortunately, the keys to those top two drawers are missing, though I have no idea how they became separated from the chest itself. The locks will be identical, of that we can be sure. The locksmith originally would have made two keys, one a replica of the other. One of these would be kept safely as a spare in case the first key got lost. One going missing is common enough, but normally a copy of the spare would be made before that could go missing, too. It is very unusual, therefore, for both keys to go missing. If I didn't know better, I would almost have to conclude that they had been deliberately lost, or even thrown away - though I can think of no reason why this should be so: these are beautiful pieces, in very good condition. I cannot imagine the last owners being careless with their keys, given how well they looked after their furniture. Equally I cannot imagine why they should deliberately dispose of them. Tragically they both died within a few weeks of each other, so I never got to ask them about it. All I know about them is that there were Army people, and had done a lot of travelling in their younger days, especially in North Africa and the Middle East. They had no children or family and so a solicitor dealt with their estate. He asked me to take their furniture, which I did gladly. These two pieces are all I have left."

So that's it, thought Pandora! They didn't want anyone ever to be able to get at what was inside the drawer. So they deliberately got rid of the only way of opening it. And they took their secret to the grave. Pandora became even more determined. She was going to find out what was inside. She would get a key from somewhere.

"Further, the two drawers are part of a sealed compartment," continued Mr. Brewster. "There is no way to get at them without taking the furniture completely to pieces. That, of course, I would never do. So I've not been able to check inside the drawers themselves. I don't think they'll have woodworm or rot as the rest of the cabinet is in such a good condition, though I normally like to check.

"Sadly for you, young lady," concluded Mr. Brewster, "it means you will not be able to use those two drawers if you and your father decide to purchase these pieces. I am sorry about that, but there is nothing I can do to open them."

"Because of the missing keys, Pandora, Mr. Brewster has taken a great deal of money off the price," added her dad. "Other people have refused the pieces once they found out two of the drawers couldn't be opened. This is why he is reducing them so much for us. It means if you want them, Pandora, they are yours."

"Though I would understand entirely if the missing key was going to be a problem," said Mr. Brewster. "I do have other pieces for you to look at, if you'd care to, though admittedly nothing as beautiful as these. Or that goes as well with yellow curtains," he added with a broad smile.

It took no time at all for Pandora to make her response.

"No, the missing key isn't a problem," replied Pandora. "Honestly. I'll manage without those two drawers, Mr. Brewster. There's plenty of room in the other three."

She turned to her dad. "The wardrobe and chest of drawers are just what I want. They are perfect. Can I have them, please?"

Pandora's dad beamed with pleasure. "Of course, Pandora," he declared. Mr. Brewster clapped his hands together in delight. Pandora tried to look far less excited than she actually felt inside, though she couldn't stop herself letting out a little yelp of delight.

After a few final pleasantries, Mr. Brewster and Pandora's dad shook hands. They went down the stairs and made their way to the counter. Pandora's dad paid the young woman at the desk. Mr. Brewster called to an assistant, also dressed in a brown overcoat, and together they carried the furniture out of the shop. They lifted it expertly into the back of Mr. Mower's van. Once it was carefully secured, Pandora's dad started the engine. Mr. Brewster said he hoped Pandora would enjoy her new furniture. Pandora said that she was sure she would. Dad and Pandora then set off for home.

As they drove along Pandora's dad chatted contentedly. He seemed really pleased to have got something that Pandora was happy with, especially with the fuss she had been making recently about Lucy's furniture coming from IDEA. He said it would be best to store the pieces in their big garden shed until the removal men came on Wednesday. There was no room for them in the house at the moment with all the packing boxes. Dad told Pandora they would be quite safe in the shed. The door had a lock and bolt. He also said he would rather Pandora didn't go near them too often - except to show it to Lucy, of course - as the shed would be very full before the move. He didn't want Pandora to knock anything over and accidentally damage either the wardrobe or the chest of drawers.

Pandora was nodding and making all the right responses from the passenger seat, but in truth she wasn't listening to anything her dad was saying. She was focussed on something else altogether. Her mind was totally absorbed by one thought and one thought alone: how to find a key for the two locked drawers.

4

Pandora's Dad and Mr. Mower got the furniture out of the van with considerably more puffing and blowing and 'to-me-to-you-ing' than when Mr. Brewster and his assistant had loaded it. To move it to the shed took them ages. Rather than carry it straight through the house, which Pandora's mum insisted would be easier, they decided to take it round the back and into the shed that way. This meant they first had to carry the furniture from the van to the end of the terrace, then down the narrow cutting that gave access to the rear alleyway, before making their way along the path between the two rows of back-to-back houses to Pandora's garden. Pandora held the back gate open for them whilst Mum watched the goings on from the kitchen window. Several times the two men lost their tempers and used some words they didn't think Pandora could hear. Finally, and with great relief, they squeezed the furniture into the shed and slammed the door shut.

When the wardrobe and chest of drawers were safely stored away, Pandora's mum made Mr. Mower and her dad a fresh cup of tea. They stood together in the kitchen drinking and chatting about the move. Pandora cringed with embarrassment while she drank her orange juice. Mum was still in her nightie and gaping dressing gown. She didn't seem to care who saw her. As soon as she had finished and put her glass into the sink, Pandora ran to call on Lucy.

Lucy lived on a smart road of detached houses a couple of streets away from Pandora's house. For many years Lucy and Pandora had lived next door to each other in the terrace. Lucy had moved when her dad had got promoted and her mum had returned to work in the library on the High Street. Lucy and Pandora were best friends.

Lucy had only just come back from her Saturday swimming lesson when Pandora arrived. Her long brown hair was still wet and her light blue t-shirt was stained dark across the shoulders. Unlike Pandora's mum, Lucy's mum was fully dressed, like always, in an immaculately smart blouse and skirt.

"We got them," said Pandora eagerly. She and Lucy were in Lucy's spotlessly clean fitted kitchen eating a chocolate biscuit. "They will look great in my new yellow bedroom."

"Has your dad said it can be yellow, then?" asked Lucy, spilling crumbs on the breakfast bar as she spoke. She wiped them up before her mum, who was frothing the milk for a cappuccino, could spot them and say something.

"Not yet," admitted Pandora, "but he has to now we have the furniture. Yellow is the only colour in the whole world that will go with them. You should have seen the way they matched the yellow curtains at the Furniture Emporium."

"Can I come and see them?" asked Lucy, catching Pandora's excitement. Lucy knew that Pandora had wanted new furniture delivered in a van and wrapped in cellophane, like hers, because Pandora had said so. Lucy was thrilled - and greatly relieved - at how happy Pandora seemed with the pieces she and her dad had found at the Furniture Emporium. Lucy had never been there. Her mum and dad only ever bought new things, and then changed them pretty quickly for something else. Lucy often felt guilty at having more money than Pandora. She didn't always tell her everything her parents bought in case Pandora got jealous and stopped being her best friend.

"Yes," said Pandora. "Of course, you can. Dad has put it in the shed until the men come on Wednesday."

When Lucy's mum went out of the kitchen to have her drink and read a magazine, Pandora beckoned to Lucy with her finger. The girls huddled together. Pandora lowered her voice so Lucy's mum wouldn't hear.

"The chest of drawers has a secret, Lucy," she whispered. "And I'm going to find out what it is."

"What sort of secret?" asked Lucy, nibbling a little more of her biscuit.

"Something is hiding inside one of the drawers." Pandora spoke dramatically, emphasising every word for maximum effect. "It is something that most definitely should not be there. And it is something nobody else but me knows anything about."

Lucy gasped and spluttered in shock and horror. Crumbs flew everywhere. It was just the sort of reaction Pandora had hoped for.

"I heard a mysterious sound coming from deep inside one of the drawers when I was alone in the shop," Pandora continued. "I'm going to find out what is making it."

Lucy put her hand over her mouth. She was not half as brave as Pandora.

"B-B-But, P-Pandora!" she stammered, her eyes widening as if they were curtains being thrown back on a sunny day. "You can't really mean that. It could be something *really* scary - like mutant mice or space aliens or giant cockroaches or...anything. I saw a film once, Pandora, where a woman heard a scratching and banging noise in her kitchen. She undid the door and switched on the light, because she thought it was her cat sharpening its nails on the doorpost. She was going to tell it off for not using the claw sharpening post-thing she had bought, when she saw this *two-headed crocodile* with massive jaws and nostrils and everything. It was eating the leftovers from a chicken casserole that she had just had for her tea. You see, the woman lived in a wooden shack near this damp and foggy swamp in which was a secret nuclear test plant that had leaked radiation into the river and..."

"Whatever it is, I think we can safely assume it not a crocodile, Lucy, and certainly not one that has been subject to radiation poisoning," interrupted Pandora, sounding, as she often did at moments like this, just like their teacher, Miss Watkins. "After all, they are only little drawers."

With that, and before Lucy could come up with any more suggestions of what might be inside the drawer, Pandora told Lucy everything that had happened inside the Furniture Emporium.

"The problem," she concluded, "is that the key is missing and Mr. Brewster thinks the lock is too old to have a new one made. So the biggest challenge is to find a way of actually opening the locked drawer."

"Couldn't you break the drawer open with a crowbar?" asked Lucy. "In 'Dangerous Diamond' this man used one to rescue the priceless necklace of a foreign princess who was in hiding working as a nanny to some children who lived in a castle in Bavaria. The butler wanted to marry her, though he didn't know at this point she was a princess, and so he thought he'd rescue her stolen necklace as a way of winning her heart. He only found out later she was a princess, though she still married him in the end. He was dead brave, Pandora.

"Well, to get the necklace he had to break into another castle down the road guarded by these men with machine guns and really fierce dogs. To get inside he had to Kung Fu loads of people, which is not something you'd normally expect of a butler. Only he was a bit more than a butler. That was the twist. You see, before he'd become a butler he'd been an undercover agent working for MI5, but had changed jobs because he was a fed up with the long hours undercover agents have to work. He used a crowbar to get the necklace out of the secret compartment of a locked drawer. He had it sewn into his jacket pocket all the time - left over from his time as an agent - though it must have stuck into him a bit when he was Kung Fu-ing everyone and climbing up the rope he had attached to exactly the right window using a mini-crossbow he had hidden in his trouser leg. Using the crowbar it only took him about a zillionth of a microsecond to open the drawer and rescue the necklace.

"Why don't you use a crowbar on your drawer, Pandora?" she ended breathlessly. "It looks ever so easy."

"Because Dad would go completely mental if he found the drawer smashed to pieces, especially as we've only just bought it," replied Pandora. "And I've have to explain why I'd attacked the new furniture with a crowbar. Anyway, where can I find a crowbar? I suppose Mr. Mower has one, but if I ask to borrow it he'll want to know why. You know what adults are like."

Lucy nodded. She knew very well.

"No," said Pandora with resolve, "I've got to find a key from somewhere, one that is exactly the right size and shape. The only question is from where."

In a flash Lucy's eyes lit up like someone had set fire to her toes.

"Of course! One of them might fit!" she exclaimed, grabbing a confused Pandora by the hand and pulling her out of the kitchen. "Come with me."

Lucy led Pandora upstairs to her bedroom. When they were inside she closed the door and made Pandora sit down on her floor. From under her bed she pulled out a box, about the size of a shoebox. It was made of wood and had the letters 'L.M.D.' carved neatly into the top.

"When she was a girl this was my grandmother's special box," explained Lucy. "The letters stand for Lucy Margaret Dawson, the name she had before she married my grandfather. Just after we moved here she gave the box to me. She never had a daughter of her own, only two boys - my dad and my uncle. Inside are the things she collected as a girl, her really precious things. She told me she didn't think her boys would be interested in them, as all they ever collected was bruises. So she saved them for her granddaughter, if ever she had one. When she thought I was old enough she gave the box to me.

"Inside," continued Lucy, "are some amazing things. There are different size brass buttons - including one from a Victorian policeman's uniform - a silver ring which used to have a pearl on it, some shells from a tropical island and a picture postcard from North Africa my grandfather sent to her when he was in the army. Mum says none of them are worth very much money. She knows because she had them valued when she wanted a new washing machine."

Pandora was just about to butt in and say that this was all very interesting, and she was glad that Lucy had them, but what had it got to do with the noise she heard inside the drawer, when Lucy got to the point.

"There are also lots of keys, Pandora, of all shapes and sizes. Most of them are very old. Some of them must be as old as your furniture. My granny collected keys. Some she found, others she was given. A few came from the printers where her father worked. One even came back with my grandfather from North Africa after the war. He picked it up in the middle of the desert and thought it might be lucky, as it was a very odd place for a key to be left lying about. Granny told me she remembered having to fetch the box out of the attic to put that key in with all the rest and how it reminded her of her collecting days when she was a girl.

"She told me she collected the keys when she was younger in case she ever came across a box of buried treasure and needed a key to open it. Granny never found any treasure, but she still kept the keys when she grew up, just in case.

"One of them might fit your drawer, Pandora," she concluded.

Though Lucy was by no means the brightest girl in their class, Pandora had to admit this was a brilliant suggestion. She nodded her approval.

Lucy undid the lid of the box. She carefully tipped out the contents onto the carpet between where the girls were sitting. Quickly they sorted the keys from everything else. They placed them to one side. The other things they put back inside the box.

Pandora waited while Lucy counted out the keys. There were over fifty. Some of them were rusty and worn; others appeared to be new and unused. All of them had interesting and unusual shapes. Each of them seemed to be unique. Some of them were made of brass. Others were coloured silver. They were so different from modern keys, most of which look as if they have been made by the same machine in the same factory.

The girls spent some time arranging the keys into groups. When they had done this, Pandora chose four brass keys that appeared to be about the same age and shape as the lock, including the one Lucy's Grandad had found in the desert. These Pandora wrapped tightly inside her hankie. She stood up and put the package into the front pocket of her jeans. Meanwhile, Lucy returned the rest of the keys to the box. This she slipped neatly back under her bed. Then Lucy also stood up.

"I wonder if one of these might just be the one, Lucy," said Pandora meditatively, patting her pocket as she spoke. "Let's go and see if any of them fit, shall we?"

5

Mr. Mower had left by the time Pandora and Lucy reached Pandora's house. His van was back in its usual place further up the terrace. Pandora's mum was having yet another rest. This time she had her feet up in front of the TV. An empty mug was balanced unsteadily on her mountainous stomach. From the ends of her toes dangled a pair of fluffy purple slippers. She was still not dressed, even though it was now mid-morning. Inside, Pandora groaned.

In answer to their question, phrased as innocently as possible, Pandora's mum told the girls that Pandora's dad had nipped out to the shops. He needed more sticky tape to seal the banana boxes he was busily packing. Pandora and Lucy glanced sideways at one another. It was a perfect opportunity to slip into the shed and try the keys in the lock. They made Pandora's mum a fresh mug of tea and found two jam tarts to keep her busy. Leaving Pandora's mum to wallow like a whale beached on the settee, the girls made their way out of the kitchen and into the small, sun-drenched rear garden.

The shed was massive, much bigger than a normal shed. Pandora's dad had bought it when, for a brief period, he had kept homing pigeons. This was why there were small air holes along the top of the four wooden walls, directly under the roof overhang, and mesh on the inside of windows that fully opened. It had been a very short-lived hobby. Pandora's dad had given it up in complete despair when not one of the pigeons he entered in his first three races came back home. Dad had put it down to them living near a flight path and the pigeons being disoriented by the sight and sound of the aircraft. Pandora and her mum thought he had just bought the wrong sort of pigeons.

Though the shed was enormous, there wasn't much room inside now the bedroom furniture was in there along with everything else. Pandora's dad and Mr. Mower had wedged the wardrobe and chest of drawers between the lawnmower that always smelt of petrol, and only worked when it felt like it, and Pandora's bike, with the puncture that her dad still hadn't fixed even though she had moaned about it for ages.

"When we go inside," instructed Pandora in a low voice, "we will have to whisper to each other. I don't want whatever is in the drawer to hear us talking. I want to be able to open the drawer without it realising. The element of surprise will be crucial."

"Can we use sign language?" asked Lucy.

"I suppose so," replied Pandora.

"Brilliant," said Lucy, "because I saw this film once where these two men were trapped behind enemy lines with only one gun and three bullets between them. They had to blow up an enemy garrison so that they could make it to safety. Well they had to use this dead secret sign language, in codes and everything, because the enemy captain saw them with his binoculars..."

"Another time, thank you Lucy," said Pandora.

"I was only going to say that it is really important to know what sort of sign language to use because these two men...," pressed Lucy.

"We'll make it up as we go along," said Pandora decisively.

It was oppressively hot and stuffy inside the shed, even with the air holes. Using the complete range of signs and gestures at her disposal Lucy pleaded with Pandora to have the windows open. Pandora refused point blank. She signed back that she didn't want her mum or dad or anyone coming along the alleyway to hear what they were doing. Pandora insisted on having the door closed, too. Lucy waved her arms as silently as she could to protest, that, if this was the case, then she definitely going to die of suffocation, and that her mum would be really cross with Pandora if she did because they had a barbecue to go to at Auntie Pam's that afternoon, and that it wasn't as hot as this when they had gone on holiday last summer to Majorca, when she had got heat rash, which hurts like mad and needs special anti-itch cream, and means you can't go in the swimming pool because of the chemicals. Pandora, however, held her ground. She was determined that the door and windows should stay closed.

"I don't want whatever is in the drawer to escape," she whispered, reverting for a moment to speech and pointing meaningfully at the drawer. "And I certainly don't want anyone to come nosing around whilst we open the drawer. We'll just have to put up with the heat."

Lucy began to mouth back that she could quite understand why the pigeons never came back to this particular shed if these were the conditions they were expected to live in. Pandora halted her abruptly with an animated command that Lucy had no difficulty in interpreting. When Pandora had composed herself again, the two girls knelt down and put their ears close against the chest of drawers. Pandora motioned to Lucy to be absolutely quiet while they listened. Lucy obeyed. The girls listened together in silence for a full two minutes. No sound could be heard anywhere inside.

"Whatever is in there must be asleep," whispered Pandora. "It must be tired after all the bumping around this morning."

"Or it has died of severe heat stroke," replied Lucy as quietly as she could. "It probably can't live in temperatures above a thousand degrees."

Pandora silenced Lucy with a withering look, the one she usually kept reserved for Billy Harper when he called her names. Then she stood up, taking special care not to kick over the toolbox on the floor. Pandora took the hankie out of her pocket and placed the four keys one at a time onto Lucy's outstretched hand.

"Please be careful, Pandora," said Lucy softly, looking at the keys in her hand. She had suddenly become very anxious about what they were doing. She nodded towards the drawer. "Are you really sure about this? You know: opening the drawer."

Pandora nodded back that she was sure, though Lucy's sudden attack of anxiety was infectious. For a brief moment it crossed Pandora's mind to wait till her dad got back from the shops and tell him everything that had happened. She quickly dismissed the thought. Pandora was determined to open the drawer and find out what was inside, and to do so with only her and Lucy present. When Pandora was determined to do something, nothing could get in her way.

Lucy watched as Pandora took a deep breath to steady herself and then selected a key from Lucy's sweaty palm.

"Here we go," she mouthed. "No going back now."

Pandora placed the key in the lock of the left hand drawer, the one nearest to her. The key slid easily into the hole. The girls looked at each other fleetingly. A mixture of excitement and fear gripped them both. Gently, so as not to make any noise, Pandora tried to turn the key.

To their frustration and disappointment, though, the key refused to move. Pandora tried turning a bit harder, in case the lock was stiff. Still the lock refused to open.

"It's not this one," said Pandora quietly. "It's the wrong key."

Pandora let go of the key and wiped both her hands down the front of her jeans. She was sweating profusely. Her hands were soaking wet and not just because the shed was so hot.

"We'll try another key," she whispered. "I'll take this one out."

Pandora took hold of the key that was still in the lock and began to pull on it gently. It stubbornly resisted her tug. She pulled harder. It would not budge. Pandora tried even harder, all the time trying to make as little noise as possible. But still there was no movement. She tried as hard as she dare without wobbling the drawer. Nothing happened. The key was totally stuck, as often happens when the wrong key is forced even a little way in a lock.

Pandora looked at Lucy. "It's stuck," she mouthed.

"What are we going to do?" replied Lucy.

"There's only one thing we can do," whispered Pandora. "It has got to come out."

Pandora took as firm as grip as she could on the key. Lucy put her hand over her mouth. With a heave Pandora began to wriggle and jiggle the key like mad, pulling and pushing, twisting and turning the key at one and the same time. Finally, after several seconds of shuddering and juddering, the key broke free.

For a second or two, the girls held their breath. Then they put their ears against the chest of drawers and listened hard. Pandora had made lots of noise and had shaken the chest of drawers around considerably. Neither girl wanted whatever was inside to wake up before the drawer had been opened.

"Phew! It must be still asleep," said Pandora after a short while. She sounded mightily relieved.

"Or dead, like I said," offered Lucy under her breath.

Pandora pretended not to hear. Instead she wrapped the first key inside her hankie and returned it to her pocket. She was about to take a second key from Lucy when she was stopped in her tracks by a mumbled sound. Pandora recognised it instantly. It seemed much louder in the confines of the shed than it had done in the large, airy room at the Emporium. But it was exactly the same sort of sound that she had heard earlier.

More than that, this time what she heard was not simply a noise. It was unmistakably... *a voice!* Further, it was trying to be as quiet as

Pandora and Lucy were. Whatever was inside obviously knew they were there and didn't want to be overheard!

Lucy heard the voice, too. At the sound she went absolutely rigid, and her face turned ashen. A scream froze on her bloodless lips. Lucy instinctively grabbed Pandora's hand. She pulled Pandora towards her, so that the two of them withdrew deeper into the shed and further from the drawer.

"Did you hear that, Pandora?" squeaked Lucy eventually. "I heard something! I cross my heart I did. Something is inside that drawer. And it's talking to itself!"

Lucy paused for a moment. "It must have gone mad, Pandora, being alone in the dark. It probably spends all its time now talking to itself. That's what the man did in *'Dungeon of Doom'*. He had been left to starve in a dungeon where there were loads of skeletons and things. Before he went mad he made friends with a mouse who lived in the dungeon. He called it Sir Roderick and taught it how to stand on its back legs while he whistled sea shanties. Eventually he began talking to himself. One day, when the guards came to see if he was dead..."

Lucy could tell Pandora was about to interrupt so she quickly returned to the point.

"You can't have drawers in your bedroom with something inside that keeps on talking to itself all the time. You won't get any sleep, Pandora. I mean, what if whatever is in there has gone nocturnal? The night-time might be when it's most active. You'll be a zombie within a fortnight."

She paused again, as a ghastly thought thrust its way into her head. "And what if your mum and dad hear the voice late at night? Or if they hear you telling it to be quiet? They'll think you've gone mad if they hear you talking to a drawer."

Lucy's mouth dropped open as an even more awful thought barged its way past the previous one.

"They might have you taken in an unmarked ambulance to The Grange, Pandora," she spluttered, "and make you live with people who think they are Queen Victoria or Elvis Presley or a banana split. Then I'll only be able to visit you once a month on a Sunday afternoon between 4 and 5pm, and you'll be wrapped in a straightjacket, and you won't know who I am anymore, and you'll think I'm a peanut, and ..."

"No one's going to put me in The Grange, Lucy," whispered Pandora. "Mum and Dad have enough to think about at the moment with the baby and the move. They won't hear a thing at night, especially with the drip from the ensuite and the baby crying.

"But what you have said raises another possibility, Lucy" she continued, the cogs in her brain whirring fast. "What if whatever is in there is not talking to itself? What if the sound is being made by *something* chattering to *something else*?"

"You mean there could be a gang of them!" cried Lucy under her breath.

As if in reply the sound came again. Though again it barely more than a murmur, this time what was being said was crystal clear to the girls' keenly attuned ears.

"Do you think they'll ever get it open?" asked a shrill voice.

"Not at this rate," replied another, deeper voice. "All they seem to be doing is whispering to each other."

"This better not be like the last time," added a third voice, somewhat menacingly. "He was useless."

At the sound of the third voice Lucy fumbled open the door. She yanked Pandora out of the shed and into the garden. She pulled Pandora halfway up the path before she spoke.

"Pandora, I don't like this one bit," she declared. "I really don't. They don't sell talking furniture at IDEA. Ours never says a word. It's really quiet all the time. Honestly. Though at least the wardrobe has been silent so far, I suppose. But who's to say it won't join in soon? Who knows what could be in there, too! I mean, in 'The Curse of the Alien Ironing Board' there was this ironing board that kept jabbering in a strange language every time the family tried to do the ironing. They found out after a while that the ironing board wasn't really an ironing board but a secret space transmitter linked to a Martian space ship orbiting the sky above their house You see, the family had been chosen to be observed by the Martians before they invaded earth and..."

"I told you, Lucy," exclaimed Pandora in delight. She was not listening to a word Lucy was saying. "I told you there was something in there. I was right! And there's more than one. There's a … colony!"

"Can we tell someone else now, Pandora?" pleaded Lucy. "Then they can open the drawer, not us. Perhaps we should call London Zoo. They must have the proper nets and cages and everything for catching whatever is in there. I'm sure they'll keep them all together. They must have a policy about not separating things from each other. I'm sure they'll be ever so happy."

"No, Lucy," declared Pandora. "*We're* going to find out what is in there. Nobody else but me and you. That's the whole point of me not telling Dad earlier. I don't just want to *hear* the voices Lucy. I want to *see* who - or what - is in there."

"But Pandora…" began Lucy.

"No buts," replied Pandora firmly. "I mean it. With or without you and your keys I am going to open that drawer."

From her tone Lucy knew Pandora was going to open the drawer. The last time Lucy had seen her as strong-minded as this was when Pandora had bought a new tunnel for her pet gerbil, George, and he had at first totally ignored it. Determined that George was going to enjoy the gift, one that had taken several week's pocket money to buy, Pandora had forced him back and forth through the tunnel until he got the idea of what he was supposed to do with it. Now, whenever he saw Pandora coming, George shot into the tunnel as fast as an express train.

Lucy considered the situation. If she went home, she would be abandoning her best friend to the things, whatever they were, for there was no way she was going to be able to persuade Pandora not to open the drawer by herself. If she stayed, however, the things might do something awful to them both, but at least they would be together.

Lucy made up her mind. When she spoke she sounded as if she was trying hard to be brave. Like the time she had played the Angel Gabriel in the school nativity play, fallen headfirst over the manger as she had floated on from stage left and landed on Alfie Buckley, the lead shepherd, who had been pretending to be asleep by the campfire. Whilst Mrs.Gordon, the deputy head, had taken Alfie to the sick bay with a nosebleed and severe shock, Lucy had carried on heroically to deliver her good news of great joy for all people.

"Then I'll stay with you," announced Lucy grandly. "You're my best friend, Pandora. If you are going to have your blood sucked out by vampire bats, or catch a terrible disease that hasn't been known since the time of the Egyptians, or have huge maggots bore their way into your brain whilst you are still alive, or be turned into a statue by a creature with enormous eyes that has special powers, or be zapped by a ray-gun and taken off in a spaceship to be experimented on, or..."

"Thank you, Lucy," said Pandora. "But I think that is enough of that."

Without another word, and with three keys in Lucy's hand still untried, the two girls went back inside the shed again and closed the door firmly behind them.

6

"Hello," began Pandora, bending down a little and addressing the drawer directly. "My name is Pandora and this is my best friend, Lucy."

Lucy didn't speak, though she did wave nervously at the drawer. Lucy was standing behind Pandora near the door and ready for a speedy getaway should this be necessary.

Pandora waited momentarily for whatever was inside the drawer to return her greeting. When nothing happened she tried a different tack.

"We heard you whispering together a few minutes ago, so we know you're in there." Pandora spoke loudly and very slowly, like English people do when they are on holiday and have to talk to someone foreign. "Please will you speak to me?"

Again, Pandora paused to give the things a chance to respond. The things, however, didn't say a word. Pandora was beginning to wonder what to try next to get the conversation going when the mumbling suddenly re-started from inside the drawers. She and Lucy quickly thrust their ears against the side of the chest of drawers and listened hard.

Unfortunately, the hum of the conversation from within was infuriatingly low. All the girls could make out were the words, 'It might' and, 'It's worth a try'. Then the mumbling stopped as quickly as it had started.

Pandora and Lucy slowly pulled their ears away from the drawer. They waited uneasily. Whatever was in the drawer seemed determined at this stage not to communicate with them. After some minutes Pandora turned to Lucy. She shrugged her shoulders in frustration as if to say she had absolutely no idea what to do next. Lucy was about to mouth in that case they should leave the drawer well alone and wait for Pandora's dad to come home, when the last voice they had heard speak piped up unexpectedly.

"Hello, Pandora," it said politely. "Hello, Lucy. We are very happy to meet you."

Pandora clasped her hands to her chest in excitement. Her face was beaming with triumph. "Now we're getting somewhere!" she declared in a whisper to Lucy. "This is so exciting!"

Lucy, on the other hand, did not look so sure.

"Find out some more, Pandora," she mouthed anxiously. "Ask how many of them are in the drawer. The thing said 'we'."

"And we are so pleased to meet you, too" replied Pandora. "How many of you are in there?" Pandora was speaking quite quickly now.

"There are just three of us," replied the voice.

"Do you have names?" asked Pandora, desperate to keep the flow of conversation going now it had finally got started.

There was another mumble before the voice, steady and confident, responded, "Tom, Dick and Harry. I'm Tom. Dick and Harry are the other two."

"Hello," said the other two voices simultaneously. The mix of their voices, one deep and other shrill, gave the impression they were singing their greeting in harmony.

"You see, there is absolutely nothing to be frightened of, Lucy," whispered Pandora, positively quivering with pleasure. "I think they are much more frightened of us. That's probably why they didn't say much at first. They must be very shy, that's all. They just need a little encouragement. Perhaps they haven't had anyone else to chat to for a very long time. I'm so looking forward to opening the drawer and seeing what they are."

"Don't open the drawer yet, Pandora!" warned Lucy. Her hands were cupped tightly around Pandora's ear so the things couldn't hear. "Not until we know *what* is in there. It could be aliens that have been trained as secret assassins and sent to earth on a mission to destroy all intelligent forms of life, starting with us. They might be waiting to zap us into tiny pieces with their space blaster as soon as you open the drawer. Before you go any further, find out what they are, Pandora."

"Well, I'm sure they can't be aliens," snorted Pandora, her voice rising noticeably above a whisper. She was starting to get annoyed with Lucy, who seemed to be spoiling everything.

"It's a ridiculous thing to suggest, Lucy," she declared haughtily. "For a start, if they had space blasters they would have blown open the drawer and escaped long before now. And, if they are intelligent enough to get here all the way from the other side of the universe I can't see how they could have got themselves trapped in a drawer. And..." - Pandora spoke as if this was all the proof she needed - "...they have such *sweet* names. No deadly space alien would ever be called Tom, Dick or Harry."

"Don't you believe it, Pandora," said Lucy, her voice getting louder, too. "I saw this film once where every night a really hairy werewolf with huge fangs went through the streets of London, eating people and doing all the horrible sorts of things werewolves do. Well in the daytime, the werewolf was actually a librarian called Gilbert who worked in the children's fiction section. Gilbert is a lovely name, but it didn't stop him turning into a werewolf every full moon. Sweet names mean absolutely nothing at all, Pandora. In fact, sweet names are good camouflage."

It was obvious to Pandora that Lucy wasn't going to be easily mollified. And this wasn't the time to pick an argument, though Pandora felt like one. Pandora knew there was nothing for it but to ask Lucy's question. She turned around and addressed the drawer.

"I hope you don't think she's being rude," said Pandora, trying to sound as if the question had nothing whatsoever to do with her, "but my friend would like to know whether you are deadly space aliens on a mission to destroy all intelligent forms of life, starting with us."

"Certainly not!" replied the confident voice immediately, sounding hurt. "We are nothing of the sort."

"Of course not. Sorry. *I* didn't think so," mocked Pandora, "but I had to ask."

Pandora turned to Lucy with the sort of smug smile that said, 'See, I told you'. Lucy was livid.

"You know I didn't mean you to ask them only if they were deadly aliens," she exclaimed furiously. "I meant you to ask them what they are and you know it. That way we'll find out what they intend to do to us, *if* we open the drawer. You don't know anything about the things in the drawer, Pandora. You'd be completely stupid to undo it before you do know. What if the things want to suck out our brains before they eat us alive? You'd be sorry then for being so friendly and for not finding out a bit more."

Pandora grabbed Lucy and pulled her close to her. "Keep your voice down, Lucy!" she said angrily through gritted teeth. "They can hear every word you're saying. Have you forgotten I said they were probably very shy? Any more of this and you'll ruin everything. They might be too scared ever to speak to me again."

For a few moments a frosty silence descended upon the otherwise sweltering shed. The two girls stood, arms folded, looking anywhere but at each other.

"Sorry, Pandora" whispered Lucy after a while. She spoke quietly, and had her head bent to the floor. "I don't want to spoil this. Honestly, I don't. But I'm a bit frightened, Pandora. That's why I want to know what is inside the drawer. That's all.

"Will you ask them properly this time?" she pleaded, lifting her head and looking straight at Pandora. "Please."

To Lucy's relief Pandora nodded her head in agreement. She also squeezed Lucy's hand. Pandora didn't want to fall out, either. And she did want Lucy to remain with her. Pandora composed herself. This time she framed the question properly.

"Sorry about what just happened. But my friend and I would very much like to know what you are," she said much more respectfully. "Forgive us for being so curious. But you probably won't be surprised to know that we have never before come across anything that talks hidden inside a locked drawer. To be honest, we're a bit nervous about letting you out."

Lucy mouthed a grateful 'thank you' at Pandora. Pandora smiled in return.

Deep inside the drawer the things began their furtive murmurings once more. Quick as a flash, the girls pressed their ears as close as they could against the burnished wood. Yet still they could make out nothing.

"We are socks," said the sure and confident voice finally. "And if you don't mind my asking, what else did you expect to find in a sock drawer?"

Pandora turned to Lucy. "You see," she whispered into her ear, "there's nothing to be frightened of, Lucy. It's only three socks. That's all."

Pandora hoped desperately this would pacify Lucy. After all, her dad would be back soon and she wanted to have the drawer open and closed again long before then. From Lucy's reply, however, it was clear that she was not yet convinced.

"That's what they say they are," Lucy whispered back. "But how do we know if they are telling the truth? Anyway, even if they are socks, they are still *talking socks.* Which means they aren't *normal* socks. Normal socks don't talk. At least, I've never had a pair that does and I don't know anyone else who has. Though, I did once get a pair of Christmas socks from Auntie Julie, each with a different squeak sewn into the top, so that one went 'Hee!' and the other went 'Ho!' - but I had to work the squeaks by myself.

"These are real talking socks, Pandora," Lucy continued. "Not ones with squeaks that break after just two washes, like mine did.

"And who knows what else these talking socks might do? I mean, they might be brilliant at hypnotising, with great big eyes that spin round and round and confuse you into doing anything they want you to. And..."

This time it was Pandora who, with a polite 'Excuse us for a moment, please' to the drawer, interrupted Lucy and heaved her out of the shed.

"I don't want any more of this nonsense, Lucy" began Pandora when they were down the alleyway and at a good shouting distance from the shed. Pandora had her hands on her hips. She looked and sounded exactly like Miss Watkins did the week before when she explaining about wind-power and Sam Gifford kept making trumping noises with his hand under his armpit.

"I've had enough of it, Lucy. I really have. I believe the things when they say they are socks. After all, why should they lie? What are they going to gain by telling us they are socks when they are…" Pandora thought hard for a moment "…mutant caterpillars or dwarf Martians? I mean talking socks is a strange enough thing to admit to, isn't it? Which must mean they are what they say they are. They are socks. Yes, they talk, and they probably do lots of other amazing things, too. But that's the whole point, Lucy. If they were ordinary non-talking socks we wouldn't be trying to undo the drawer, would we?

"So," she concluded with finality, "do you want come back in with me whilst I try to open the drawer, or not?"

"Of course I do," said Lucy sulkily.

"Good," said Pandora, taking her hands from her hips. "Let's go back in then, shall we? And remember, no more ridiculous questions."

With that the girls went back inside the shed and closed the door. Pandora apologised for their absence. She explained that she and Lucy had 'one or two little matters' that had needed to sort out, but that everything was fine now. Pandora stared at Lucy to make sure she had got the message.

"We've got three more keys to try in the lock," Pandora said chattily to the drawer. "Hopefully one of them will fit. I'm going to try the next one now."

"Lucy, may I have the next key?" asked Pandora.

Lucy got them ready in her outstretched hand. Carefully, Pandora chose a second key. She inserted it gently into the hole of the left hand drawer. It slipped in as easily as the first.

Pandora was just about to try the key when a dreadful thought occurred to her. Instinctively she took her hand off the key. Pandora bit her lip for a moment, hesitating whether to voice her concern out loud or keep it to herself.

"Excuse me," she said eventually. Pandora was obviously a little embarrassed about sharing her own anxiety when she had been so hard on Lucy and her worries. "I hope you don't mind my asking one last question. But it's awfully important to me that I know the answer."

There was a stony silence from the drawer. And also from Lucy, who seemed surprised that Pandora should be asking a question after all she had said to her.

"Do you promise not to run away once the drawer is opened?" asked Pandora. "I so want us to be friends. That's all."

This time there was absolutely no pause. The confident voice responded immediately.

"Of course, we promise not to run away," it replied. "Why should we want to do that?"

Pandora sighed with relief. She put her hand back on the handle of the key. Like Miss Watkins, when she was on dinner duty, Pandora was satisfied that she had the situation well under control.

7

With renewed confidence, Pandora began to turn the second key. Although she had no need this time to worry about making any noise, Pandora nonetheless worked cautiously. She desperately didn't want to get the key stuck fast in the lock. Not only would it mean she couldn't try the other two keys. It would also be difficult to explain what she had been doing to her dad without him asking some very awkward questions.

Without the slightest resistance, the key moved a tiny fraction in the lock. Pandora took her hand off it, then crossed her fingers and arms, turned around and touched her nose for luck. It was an extremely difficult manoeuvre in a crowded shed. Lucy, who had no such elaborate rituals to hand, and who was nervous about bumping into the petrol mower and getting oil on her t-shirt, simply held her breath and placed a hand across her mouth.

There was complete silence from the drawer.

After no more than an eighth of a turn, however, the key appeared to change its mind about doing a complete circle. It stubbornly refused to go further. It was well and truly jammed. In frustration Pandora muttered a very rude word, one she had heard her dad say when Wiggle, their three-legged cat, had eaten his teatime kipper whilst he had been washing his hands at the sink. Lucy looked shocked.

From inside the drawer came a loud sigh of disappointment.

"It's not this one either," said Pandora to the drawer, composing herself. "But we've still got two more to go. I'll just have to prise this one out."

With some considerable effort Pandora jiggled the key about. Finally it became loose enough to remove safely. Pandora placed it in her pocket alongside the first key. Like a nurse in an operating theatre awaiting the surgeon's instructions, Lucy dutifully held out her sweaty palm once more.

Of the two keys left, one was exceptionally shiny. It looked as if it wanted desperately to be noticed, like Ryan Richards, who always put his hand up in class and made strange grunting noises to attract Miss Watkins' attention, even though he never knew the answer. The other key, however, looked demure. It gave the impression of being extremely shy and bashful.

Pandora studied them both. She ignored the shiny one and focussed instead on the other one. Pandora slowly picked it up and examined it. The more she looked at it, the more she had the strong impression that this key had to be the one.

"That's the one Grandad found in the desert," said Lucy.

"Well, let's hope it's lucky for us," replied Pandora.

Abandoning her previous caution, and without a word to either the drawer or Lucy, Pandora slid the blade of the key inside the hole. It went in without any resistance at all. She began confidently to turn the round bow of the key anti-clockwise. As she did so, Pandora felt a surge of energy rush from her feet to her head. The lock responded effortlessly to the twisting of the key. Inside the drawer Pandora could almost hear the tumblers begin to fall away. With the key about three quarters of the way round the turn, Pandora spoke to Lucy.

"This is the one," she said breathlessly. "It's opening!"

Lucy gulped twice. Her throat was fast becoming tight and dry. Scenes from various films she had seen rushed across her eyes, each melting into the other and producing a single, terrible vision of catastrophe and doom. As the key completed the turn, the girls heard from inside the lock a loud 'click'.

They weren't the only ones to hear the sound.

"At last," shrieked the first voice, sharp and clear above the others' brief, ecstatic cheers. "Freedom!" Then, after what sounded to the girls like a series of rapid slithers, the voices fell completely silent.

Without speaking Pandora moved her trembling fingers from the key and onto the teardrop shaped handle. Slowly, little by little, she pulled open the drawer. It slid open as easily and noiselessly as an ice dancer glides across the rink. Pandora peered inside. Lucy stared over her shoulder.

Oddly, however, even though there was plenty of light pouring into the shed through the dusty window, neither girl could see anything in the drawer. It appeared to be completely empty.

"Perhaps they have fallen down the back," suggested Lucy. "At home my socks are always falling into the drawer underneath."

"I don't think they can have," said Pandora, "because Mr. Brewster said that these two top drawers are part of one single compartment, separate from the three drawers below. They might be shielding their eyes from the sunlight, given that they've been in the dark for a long time. Perhaps they've slipped into the drawer on the other side for a moment or two whilst they get used to the light again. I'll ask them where they are."

"Excuse me," she began warily, "we've opened the drawer, but we can't see you. Where are you? Are you alright?"

No reply came from anywhere in the chest of drawers. Pandora and Lucy looked at each other. Something was not right.

"Tom? Dick? Harry? Where are you?" Pandora was speaking very loud. "We can't see you anywhere. Are you alright?"

Still there was no reply. The silence was absolute.

"Do you think you might have accidentally strangled them when you opened the drawer?" asked Lucy. "They might have got their heads caught, or their necks or something."

"I can't have," replied Pandora with certainty. "I pulled it out so slowly they'd have had plenty of time to get out of the way or call out. Anyway, if I had got them caught, we'd see the socks somewhere in the drawer.

"They're either invisible," she mused, "or they are deliberately hiding."

"Why would they do that?" gasped Lucy.

"I really don't know," said Pandora. "But I intend to find out."

"Shut the drawer, Pandora," shouted Lucy, suddenly becoming fearful. "Don't leave it open. This could all be a nasty trick."

In response, Pandora slammed the drawer shut and locked it with a swift turn of the key. As the lock clicked once more and her hand fell away from the key the deep voice cried out, "Too late! She's closed it again. I told you we had to move quickly."

"What on earth are you doing?" spluttered Pandora sharply at the sound. "Why did you hide when I opened the drawer?"

But the socks weren't listening to Pandora. From deep within the drawer there arose a sudden tidal wave of raised and angry voices. The socks were arguing with each other. There was much the girls couldn't hear from the commotion being made, but they did hear quite distinctly, 'I said hiding on the other side was a stupid idea,' and, 'we should have just gone for it'. Then, as if suddenly remembering they were being overheard, the voices fell immediately silent.

"So, you had a plan to escape, did you?" cried Pandora, at once grasping their intentions. "You made me a promise! And I believed you.

"I see it all now!" she continued haughtily. "You had crawled through the gap between the two top drawers and were going to hide in the other drawer until we opened that one, too. Then you were going to escape out of the first drawer whilst we were looking inside the second one. How rude!

"Well," she declared icily, in a tone of which Miss Watkins would have been particularly proud, "at least Lucy and I now know what sort of socks we are dealing with."

"Cheats and liars," added Lucy. "The sort of socks who deserve to get a really bad dose of heat rash." She stuck out her tongue towards the drawer and twizzled her fingers inside her ears.

"Listen to me, you naughty socks" announced Pandora authoritatively, standing very still like a drill sergeant on parade. "Before we do anything more, Lucy and I are going to the house to have a drink and a biscuit. We need a private chat. We have to decide exactly what to do with you.

"You are to stay exactly where you are," she ordered. "Do you understand?"

"We're hardly likely to go anywhere else now, are we?" said the third voice in a most unpleasant manner.

"Don't worry, we'll be waiting for you, Miss Bossy Boots," squealed the first sarcastically.

Filled with a sudden fury at being called names, Pandora was about to say that she jolly well wasn't bossy, and that actually Miss Watkins had told her mum and dad at Parents' Consultations she was a very helpful girl who could be trusted with responsibility, and that on Monday she always took the dinner money to Mrs. Robertson's office, and that twice - not once, but twice - she had been 'Pupil of the Week' last term, and not even Pollyanna Pritchard had managed that, and if this was their attitude then they could stay inside the drawer for a long time whilst they thought about things, especially about whether that was a positive way to talk to the person whose bedroom they would be living in, when Lucy took her friend firmly by the arm and guided her decisively out of the shed.

8

Pandora's mum was in the kitchen, feeding Wiggle. She had finally got dressed, which was something, though, now she had, Pandora wished she hadn't bothered. If she was embarrassing in her nightie, what she was wearing now was ten times worse. She had on pink flip-flops, tight blue leggings which gripped like a vice in all the wrong places and a purple t-shirt splattered with the words, 'We went to Corfu and all I got was this lousy t-shirt'. The t-shirt, never designed to work with such a wide load, had ridden up over her bump to reveal a thick band of stretched skin. It looked like someone had spent a happy morning marble painting in pink, white and red across her gigantic belly. In the middle, like the inflamed eye of an overweight Cyclops, stuck out an enormous belly button. Pandora had never seen Lucy's mum's stomach. Pandora's dad was still out.

"Hello girls," she said cheerily. "You both look a bit hot. Make sure you don't get dehydrated. It's pretty warm out there today. Would you like something to drink?"

Pandora looked at Lucy with a 'now is not the best time to say anything about tropical sheds and heat rash' sort of look.

"Yes, please," said Lucy, taking note. "Can I have some milk?"

Pandora took out the biscuit barrel and fished down to the bottom. There were only a few digestives left, most of them broken. Mr. Mower and her dad had obviously eaten all the chocolate ones. Pandora found the two least broken biscuits, and gave one to Lucy. Her mum poured out two beakers of milk, in the process spilling a big dollop on the already heavily stained carpet tiles. With a sigh she declared she was 'too big and fat to be of any use to anyone' and waddled her way back to the TV.

"You'll understand what it's like when you're pregnant," she said cryptically over her retreating shoulder.

Wiggle hopped along the floor to mop up the spillage whilst Pandora and Lucy seated themselves at the worn kitchen table.

"What are you going to do now, Pandora?" asked Lucy once she was sure they were alone. "They obviously can't be trusted to be in your new bedroom, not even locked up. You'll never be able to believe a word they say. They are smelly, dirty liars. And I hope their pants catch fire," she added with feeling.

"I'm sorry to disappoint you, Lucy, but they probably don't wear pants," said Pandora sensibly. "They are socks. I don't think they need underwear."

"Ah! They *say* they are socks," retorted Lucy, returning happily to her favourite theme. "But how do we know? The only thing we know about them is that they tell lies. We've never seen them. They could be anything.

"In fact, for all we know they could actually be baby dinosaurs!" continued Lucy, getting into her stride once more. "Ones that have just come out of eggs found by an explorer who brought them home from an iceberg where they had been frozen.

"That's it, Pandora!" she exclaimed, as if she had suddenly found the answer they were searching for. "The explorer must have put the eggs in his sock drawer to keep them cool until he knew what to do with them. He then must have died before he had time to warn anyone of what was in there. This must be his furniture. The warmth in your shed might have made them hatch! After all, it must be the same temperature in there as in prehistoric jungle days.

Pandora scowled, but Lucy ignored her.

"Just think Pandora! By now they must be about three metres tall. They could even now be eating their way out through the shed!" Lucy's face was suddenly blanketed by a look of sheer terror. "Oh, Pandora! What if this huge dinosaur head comes through your kitchen window any minute now and..."

"Lucy," said Pandora, sounding like Miss Watkins does when she has a headache and is telling the class it is time for a spot of quiet reading, "to begin with, it is highly unlikely that baby dinosaurs have the ability to speak the moment they are born, let alone speak English. Secondly, the noise we heard in the shed is the same one I heard at Mr. Brewster's. Therefore they can't have been born since we got them home, as they must have already been alive, which means they aren't growing at the rate you suggest. So, I think we can safely cross 'dinosaur invasion' off our list of immediate concerns."

Pandora was going to add that, thirdly, if Lucy said anything else ever again about the temperature of the shed she was going to do something to her that was not on Miss Watkins' Classroom Charter, but let it go. There were more important matters to attend to at present.

"For the present, therefore," she continued briskly, "we will continue to assume they are what they say they, and that is socks. Unusual socks, I admit, but still socks."

Pandora took a big gulp of milk and licked her lips slowly. "Anyway, we'll know what they are when we open the drawer again, won't we Lucy?"

"No way!"' said Lucy firmly, crossing her arms in the way her mum did whenever her dad asked if he could go to the football match or the pub. "We are *not* opening the drawer. Not now, Pandora. I wouldn't trust those horrid things one bit after what they just did. You never know what they'll do once they see daylight again. They might bite us – we know they can speak, so they must have mouths. In fact, they probably have fangs. We could get a nasty rash, Pandora, or come out in huge red spots full of bright yellow puss, like my dad did when he used my mum's razor on his face. No. I think we should forget all about opening the drawer and tell your dad everything that has happened when he gets back from the shops."

"But we would only have a quick peep, Lucy," pleaded Pandora. "You know what will happen if an adult finds out about them before we have had a chance to see them. Once they know about the socks they won't let us anywhere near the drawer. It will be people in white coats with test tubes and goggles who see the socks first, not us.

"Just think, Lucy," she added temptingly, knowing Lucy's weak spot. "Whoever opens the drawer first could well be in the newspapers one day. After all, not everyone discovers talking socks, do they?"

Lucy didn't answer straightaway. Ever since her cousin Mollie had been photographed on the front cover of the local free weekly after winning a swimming gala she had always dreamed of being in the newspaper.

"I suppose a very quick peep might be alright," agreed Lucy cautiously. "But we'll need something to protect us from a surprise attack". She thought hard for a moment.

"I know, Pandora! I saw this film once where a huge bear was chasing this man because he had gone into its mountain cave thinking it was an abandoned goldmine. Well, the bear chased him up and down loads of passages so he got terribly lost. Just as the bear was going to grab him and crush him to smithereens, the man pointed his torch and shone it into the bear's face, blinding him for a few seconds. Then the man escaped." Lucy paused for breath.

"However, because he was so lost the man ended up further underground. Eventually, when he thought he was going to die, he sat down and dropped his torch in despair, but as it fell his torch picked out some gold in the rock so he knew he was actually in the goldmine. Then he looked around and found the original mineshaft and climbed up an old rope to the surface, and became a millionaire and was dead famous and everything." Lucy paused for another breath.

"Well, we could shine your dad's bike lamp right inside the drawer and blind them with it while we look at them. They obviously aren't used to sunlight yet. Then they won't be able to jump out and attack us."

"Brilliant idea, Lucy," said Pandora excitedly, "It will be a scientific experiment. Our first proper experiment."

"What about when we grew broad beans in blotting paper?" queried Lucy. Pandora generously did not remind Lucy that hers, in fact, did not grow, because she forgot to water them, and that they had shared Pandora's instead. "Miss Watkins said that was an experiment."

"That's not a *proper* experiment," said Pandora scornfully. "But this is. Along with the torch we will take a couple of wooden spoons, Lucy, in case they try to wriggle out. A quick whack on the head - whichever end of the sock it is - should soon stop them in their tracks."

"When will you tell the newspaper, Pandora?" asked Lucy, not wanting Pandora to forget what she had just said. "How long will you want to keep the socks a secret?"

Pandora thought about this question for quite some time.

"I don't want to say anything straight away," she said at last to Lucy's obvious disappointment. "Unless something terrible happens, or I find I can't bear them to be in my new bedroom, we'll keep this to ourselves until we are much older. Otherwise the adults will want to know why we didn't say anything in the first place and we'll get into trouble. Once we've had a look at the socks we'll lock the drawer again with your granny's key. Then, you should take her key home and put it back in your box. That way I can't undo the drawer without asking you for the key. Then we should make a solemn promise never even to think about undoing the drawers until we are say, eighteen. Then we'll tell the newspapers and reveal our discovery to the world."

"I agree," said Lucy eventually, whilst secretly thinking that she'd rather be in the newspaper sooner. "And I know the very best way to make a solemn promise.

"I saw this film once, Pandora, in which two men found some Aztec treasure in the middle of a rainforest. They were archaeologists and promised never to reveal what they had found as they wanted the treasure to stay undisturbed. So they cut into each other's palms with a huge hunting knife until the blood oozed out. Once they had done this - and they never even flinched because they were so brave - to make their promise binding they shook each other's hand. This meant the blood from one man's cut flowed into the other one's cut as they said the words. It made them blood brothers and meant they could never break their promise, not even if they were being horribly tortured to death or eaten alive by lions. We should do the same, Pandora, when we make our solemn promise! We could use your mum's bread knife and cut deep into each other's hands until the blood flows out. Then we should shake hands and make a solemn vow. It would make us blood sisters."

"Thank you, Lucy," said Pandora, "But I think we'll just adapt the Brownie promise"

With that, and before Lucy could protest or come up with another bright idea, Pandora rose to her feet and set off towards the cupboard under the stairs to find her dad's bike lamp.

As Pandora was delving around inside the cupboard looking for the lamp, Pandora's dad came in through the kitchen door. He was loaded down with shopping bags.

"Hello, Lucy," he said merrily as he plopped the heavy bags down on the table. "You look hot. Have you been running around? Mind you, I must look a bit sweaty, too. I only went out for some sticky tape, and ended up with this lot! It's a long way back from the High Street when you are a beast of burden.

"Is Pandora around?" he enquired.

"I'm in here Dad," said Pandora, her voice echoing from inside the cupboard. "Do you want me?"

"Only for a minute," said her dad, pouring himself a glass of water.

Pandora came out from the cupboard. She was holding the bike lamp. If her dad wondered why she needed it on such a bright sunny day, he didn't ask. He wasn't that sort of dad. And he clearly had something else on his mind.

"Pandora," he asked. "Have you been in the shed?"

"Why?" replied Pandora, trying to sound innocent.

"Because the door was wide open when I came in through the garden gate," he said. "I distinctly remember closing it this morning after we had put the furniture in there."

"Yes, Dad," admitted Pandora. She knew it was no good lying. "I took Lucy in there to show her my new furniture. But you did say I could."

"That's fine," he said. He was glad that Pandora wanted to show her furniture to Lucy. "I'm not telling you off or anything like that. In fact, I wanted to check it was you who had been in there so I could be sure I was congratulating the right person."

For a moment Pandora and Lucy looked totally bemused.

"Well done for finding a key to the drawers!" he exclaimed. He bent down and gave Pandora a huge kiss on the forehead. "You've been able to do something that Mr. Brewster could not do, not even with all his experience and contacts in the furniture business. In super-record time, too! I saw the key sticking out the drawer when I looked around the shed to check everything was in order. I'm really pleased for you, Pandora. It means you can use all the drawers when we move. Charlie will never be able to get at your secret things.

"Where did you get the key from?" he continued, at the same time beginning to put away some tins of cheap cat food.

"Lucy's granny collected keys, when she was a girl," replied Pandora, hoping her dad wouldn't want to ask too many questions. "She gave them to Lucy in a special box, along with all sorts of other things."

"Shells and buttons and a ring and postcards," explained Lucy. "They're all really old. Even a Victorian policeman's button."

"When I told Lucy about the drawers she remembered about the keys," continued Pandora. "We chose four we thought looked about the right size and shape. We hoped one of them might work."

"It was my idea," said Lucy. She didn't want Pandora to take all the credit. "I thought of it. It wasn't only Pandora."

"Well, that key certainly fits," said Dad, unpacking the last of the tins and packets. His back was to the girls. "I've tried it myself in both the small drawers, so I know it works."

Pandora and Lucy looked at each other. For a moment they were so overcome with total and absolute panic that they were unable to speak. The same terrible question had exploded simultaneously into their minds: did this mean Dad had found out about the socks?

From what he said next, however, it was clear he knew nothing whatsoever about their existence.

"I've brought the key with me out of the shed so it doesn't get lost," he continued. "I've also closed the shed door and pulled across the outside bolt. Here's the key, Pandora. Please put it somewhere safe. We'll see if we can get another one cut after we've settled in so we've got a spare." He gave the key back to Pandora, who slipped it quickly into her other pocket, separate from the first two keys.

"I'll tell you what, Pandora," he said, leaning back on the work-surface and folding his arms. "They don't make furniture like that anymore. When I tried those top two drawers they opened as smoothly as the others, the ones that have been in regular use. Even though they must have been locked shut for ages, they slipped in and out like they had only been waxed yesterday. That's craftsmanship, you know.

"Anyway, I'd better get back to the packing," he said, unfolding his arms and making a move towards the hallway. "Otherwise we'll never be ready for Wednesday."

Pandora and Lucy put their empty beakers into the kitchen sink. They began to make their way towards the back door. They wanted to get back to the drawers before Pandora's dad discovered anything else.

"By the way," he shouted from the hallway, just as the girls reached the back door. "I had a quick chat over the fence with Mrs. Dunstan. Honeysuckle had four puppies yesterday. She says you can pop round and see them later. Apparently three are golden and one is a sort of rusty colour. That's the one she thinks she is going to keep. She's on her way to fetch her grandchildren for the afternoon. She hopes to be back by about two o'clock and said to go round after that. Oh! One more thing, Pandora."

"What's that?" asked Pandora, her fingers resting anxiously on the door handle.

"I'd rather you not go back into the shed," he instructed. "Not now you've seen the furniture."

"Why?" called Pandora.

"Because I've left the two top drawers open to give them a bit of an air," he said, beginning to climb the stairs. "I thought they could do with it having been closed for so long. They didn't smell musty when I checked them, but I still think it's worth giving them a bit of a blow for a day or two. So I don't want you to go back into the shed just in case you catch yourselves on them. There's not much room in there now with the drawers sticking out. See you later."

As Pandora's dad's feet echoed up the stairs, the two girls stared at each other open-mouthed. Dad had left the drawers wide open. He had no idea what he had just done! Whereas they knew only too well!

9

"Don't open the door!" shouted Pandora as she and Lucy reached the shed. "They might not have got away. Dad made certain the door fitted really tight to stop his pigeons escaping. Unless the socks nipped out when Dad wasn't looking, they must still be inside."

The girls peered breathlessly through the dusty window. Directly opposite was the wardrobe and chest of drawers. As Pandora's dad had said, the top two drawers were fully open. From where Pandora and Lucy stood they looked to be completely empty. Inside them could be seen no trace of any sock.

Pandora and Lucy quickly scanned their eyes around the shed. Along with the wardrobe and the now empty chest of drawers they could see all sorts of things: toolboxes, half used tins of paint, bikes, the lawnmower, assorted garden tools, beach games and a fishing net for the rock pool, the barbeque with the wobbly leg that Dad insisted was still safe, and the body board that Pandora had bought on holiday last year, and which had lost its wrist strap on the roof rack on the journey home.

But they could not see anywhere the one thing they were desperately hoping to see: three talking socks.

Turning their backs to the shed, Pandora and Lucy slumped down to the ground. Pandora pulled her knees up under her chin. They sat for a while in gloomy silence. Pandora was in no doubt that this was far more serious than when Jack Proctor had trapped Henry Martin in the boy's toilets because he had been messing around with the lock and

Mr. Billings, the caretaker, had been forced to spend the whole of lunch hour getting him out.

Pandora had absolutely no idea what to do. She was about to ask if Lucy had ever seen a film where something like this had happened, when a tinny tapping sound from inside the shed brought the girls swiftly to their feet.

Nervously, they peered through the window. There, on top of the chest of drawers, were three socks. One was light blue, another bright red and the third one a glorious emerald green. Puncturing the toe part of the socks were two piercing black eyes, all as dark as the bottom of a very deep well. Each had a slim black mouth that looked as if it had been drawn with a thin felt tip pen. Protruding from each slender mouth was a pair of razor sharp fangs. This sinister countenance made them look more like snakes than socks, an impression that was confirmed as soon as the girls saw the socks move.

Also on top of the chest was a tin of bright pink paint, one that hadn't been there a few moments before. The green sock had wrapped itself like a coil around the tin. From its thin mouth an even thinner tongue darted rapidly in and out between its shiny white fangs. The blue sock held the shaft of a screwdriver between its fangs. It had placed the pointed end under the lip of the lid and was holding the wooden end towards the red sock. The red sock was tapping the end of the screwdriver with a hammer gripped tightly in its mouth. When the socks saw the girls peering through the window they stopped what they were doing, and fixed them with a stony black gaze.

Noiselessly, the green sock unwrapped itself from the tin. It slithered down the chest of drawers, across the shed floor and up the leg of the barbeque. The sock pulled itself up until its unmoving eyes were only millimetres from theirs on the other side of the pane of glass. It hissed hideously, revealing as it did so sparkling drops of saliva dripping from its fangs. Then the green sock spoke in a soft and yet peculiarly menacing voice. The girls recognised it immediately as the first voice they had heard from inside the drawer.

"Hello," it leered. "Have you come to watch the fun?"

With that it slowly spat out its tongue, turned and slithered silently back to the top of the drawer. The sock wrapped itself once more around the tin of paint.

"Are you ready, boys?' asked the green sock. "Good. I've got it tight. Let's get the lid off!"

At his command the red sock began to tap the end of the screwdriver. The girls watched horrified as each blow gradually prised open the lid of the tin.

"Oh no!" cried Pandora. "My new bedroom furniture! The paint will ruin it. Dad will go ballistic!"

Pandora darted from the window to the shed door. Without thinking, she drew back the outside bolt. Then she grabbed the handle and yanked open the door.

"Stop that at once!" she shouted furiously from the open doorway. "And get back inside the drawer!"

It was exactly what the socks had wanted. At the green sock's signal the other two socks opened their jaws and dropped the tools. Then together, like squashed springs that had been suddenly released, the three socks sprang off the chest of drawers and hurtled straight towards Pandora.

It all happened so fast that Pandora had no time whatsoever to get out of their way. The three socks crashed headfirst - or rather foot first - into her stomach. Like a boxer who had been caught off guard by a surprise blow Pandora crumpled instantly. She was completely winded by the force of the impact. Fighting for her breath she clenched her stomach and collapsed in a heap on the floor. Through the doorway and over her writhing and gasping body wriggled three streaks of colour - red, blue and green - as they slithered their way out into the garden.

"That was so-o-o-o easy-peasy-lemon-squeezy," jeered the green sock, stopping briefly to hiss into Pandora's ear. Then, with a spiteful flick of its tail, one that caught Pandora directly in the eye, it was gone.

As the green sock disappeared under the garden fence Lucy rushed to Pandora's side. "Where does it hurt?" she asked anxiously. "Do you want me to fetch your mum? Shall we tell your dad what's happened?"

"I'll be fine in a minute," sobbed Pandora. With Lucy's help she struggled to her feet. She rubbed her tummy with one hand and her stinging eye with the other. "Don't get Mum. I don't want her to know anything. Nor Dad.

"We've got to get the socks back first, Lucy" she said defiantly, as her tears burned angrily into her cheeks. "Or else there will be big trouble."

10

"We've got to capture them before they get too far away," declared Pandora, each moment sounding more like her old self. The wind was fast coming back into her sails, bringing with it a fresh resolve.

"How on earth are we going to do that?" exclaimed Lucy. "I mean, they move so fast. It's like they were jet propelled. They were out of the shed and over you like three rockets. I think they went off in different directions, too. There is no telling where they could be by now." She paused for a moment. Pandora knew exactly what was coming.

"I saw this film once, Pandora, where some jungle explorers captured this huge boa constrictor in the Amazon. It kept eating the local villagers, which they didn't like very much, so they were glad to get rid of it. Anyway, the explorers gave it to a zoo, but it escaped when the keeper left the door open. Well, no one knew where it was for ages, though they sent out search parties and helicopters with lights and police cars and submarines and everything.

"Eventually, the police found out that the boa was in a soup factory. It had kept itself alive by eating soup when people were on their tea breaks and things, so no one ever saw it slithering around the factory floor. The police only found out where it was when they made the connection between the boa and why people all over the country kept returning tins of leek and potato soup to the supermarkets, complaining they were only half full, like someone had eaten the other half already. It took a brilliant detective to make the link between the soup and the snake, though no one else had realised quite how brilliant a detective he was until then, as his normal job was to file parking tickets.

"No one would believe the brilliant detective at first because they would not believe the boa had become a vegetarian. Of course, that was the whole point of the boa's clever disguise, which is very smart for a snake. You see, everyone thought the boa would have gone for chicken and mushroom or oxtail, or even winter broth, which I think personally is like drinking hot sick.

"Well, the film ended with this utterly brilliant detective laying this dead clever trap. He took a huge fishing rod and hung loads of fresh leeks and potatoes from a line. The he got this police helicopter to keep flying around the factory while he dangled the leek and potatoes near windows and pipes and vents and things. After a while the boa, who had by now given up meat altogether and become totally addicted to vegetables, caught the scent and followed the smell of the fresh leeks and potatoes out of the factory and into this specially constructed pit near some road works by a motorway bridge

"We could try something like that," concluded Lucy triumphantly. "If it worked for the boa, it could work with the socks."

Lucy looked at Pandora expectantly, like she had come up with a really good suggestion of how to recapture the socks. The moment was very short lived.

"Thank you very much, Lucy," said Pandora sarcastically. She sounded just like Miss Watkins when she discovered that Bernie O'Leary had erased her name and inserted 'Miss Spotkins' on the front of the class register just before the Ofsted Inspector arrived to observe them for the morning.

"Unfortunately, that doesn't help us much does it? Why, you ask? Well, your brilliant plan has one major weakness. You see, I don't think these socks need food to survive. They seem to have lasted quite well locked in the drawer until now without it. So, I don't think we'll be spending the rest of the afternoon setting traps of fresh vegetables or even using tins of soup. Do you?

"But I do think it will be very helpful, Lucy," she added, "If you are completely quiet for a moment while *I* think of what to do next."

Pandora folded her arms in frustration and leaned against the side of the shed. She didn't get long to think, however, before Lucy exploded into speech.

"You can't say that we might not need tins of soup later," she complained angrily, "because the socks might develop a taste for it. You aren't always right about everything, Pandora Johnson. After all, the boa became a vegetarian when no one expected it to. These socks might suddenly want some soup. Or ice cream. Or prune juice. Or even raspberry jelly. So, it might turn out to be a good idea in the end. In fact, I think it will. Then you'll have to thank me and say I'm as brilliant as that detective.

"Anyway," she said with satisfaction, "you don't even know where they are so you don't know any better than me how to capture them."

"It looks like they are much closer than you think, Lucy," whispered Pandora slowly. She wasn't looking at Lucy. Instead, she was staring intently over Lucy's shoulder. Lucy turned her head and followed the line of her gaze up the garden path.

From the small window above the sink in Pandora's kitchen, milk had begun to splash like a creamy waterfall onto the patio below. When the flow of milk stopped an empty carton whizzed out of the window. It landed in a flowerpot in Mrs. Holland's garden next door. Then a fresh supply of milk began to flow once more. At the sound of the splashing Wiggle hopped his way through the cat flap, his single front leg appearing first as if it were an antennae. Lazily he began to lick up the milky lake.

"Dad's shopping!" shouted Pandora. "He won't like that one bit! He hates food shopping at the best of times. But at least we know where one of them is. It must have got in through the cat flap."

The girls ran as fast as they could up the garden path. They pulled open the back door and looked around. Thankfully, the door from the kitchen to the hallway was closed thereby sealing the room from the rest of the house. From upstairs they could hear the stomp of Pandora's dad's feet as he packed and the throb of the music from the radio show he was listening to. Pandora's mum was laughing at something on the TV in the front room. Neither had heard anything from the kitchen.

The blue sock was in front of the open fridge. It had a carton of milk in its mouth. When it saw the girls the sock dropped the carton onto the floor. It hissed at them in a sinister way, its jet-black tongue darting in and out of its sly mouth.

"Well, hello," it squeaked in a high-pitched voice. "I rather thought I was going to be all on my own. As you can see, the fun is just beginning."

With a sickening smile the sock abandoned the fridge. It slithered speedily up a cupboard and onto a crowded work surface. Deliberately crashing into storage jars and containers, scattering their contents in its wake, the sock heaved open one of the cupboards with its sharp fangs. It began throwing the contents out of the cupboard in a venomous frenzy. Packets of cereal and cheese sauce and gravy and flour and pasta and rice and herbal tea (for when Mum got trapped wind, which she often did being pregnant) began to rain down like cannonballs on the temporarily stunned and shocked girls.

Pandora was roused out of her stupor when a bag of Californian raisins hit her straight between the eyes. Quick as a flash she grabbed the biscuit barrel, one of the few things the sock hadn't so far overturned, and yanked off the lid. Pandora looked inside. Since returning from the shops Dad had filled it to the brim with delicious looking chocolate cookies. It was tragic to waste them, especially as the girls had earlier had only a mouldy old digestive, but there was nothing else for it. Pandora tipped the contents onto the floor. For a split second it looked to Lucy like Pandora had gone insane and was helping the sock to ransack the kitchen.

Lucy was just about to scream out for Pandora's mum and dad to come and put an end to the fury and madness when, upturned biscuit barrel in one hand and lid in the other, Pandora lunged at the sock.

She caught it completely off guard. The sock was too absorbed in emptying the cupboards to notice a sudden attack from behind. With the speed and skill of a professional basketball player doing a spectacular slam-dunk, Pandora brought the open barrel crashing down on top of the sock. In one swift movement she trapped it inside. Her aim and technique were so good that, had the moment been caught on camera, it would almost certainly have won Pandora a nomination for Sports Personality of the Year.

Once she was certain she had the sock totally secure, Pandora dragged the upturned biscuit barrel along the work surface, being careful not to lift it by even a fraction. When she had the biscuit barrel right at the edge Pandora put the lid of the biscuit barrel as close to the work surface as she could. Then, in a movement as fast as that made by the socks a short time before, she brought the biscuit barrel off the work surface and down onto the lid. Pandora turned the biscuit barrel the right way round, pressed down the lid and put the sealed container on the floor.

"Quick, Lucy! Sit on this," she commanded, flicking some stray hair out of her eyes.

"But what if it bites my bottom?" protested Lucy. "I won't be very happy about that, Pandora, and nor will my mum. Those socks have really sharp fangs. I bet they can bite through anything and that biscuit barrel isn't reinforced against fangs. It could be just like 'Razor Sharp and Deadly'. In that film this man had his leg bitten right off by this enormous shark that chewed through the bottom of his rowing boat. The man told his son to hold together the shark's jaws because the shark had got his leg still in its mouth and he didn't want it chewing up in case it could be stitched back on later. While his son held the shark's mouth, the man hopped on his one good leg over an erupting volcano to get help from a missionary doctor who he knew was in a village seventeen kilometres away on the other side of a swamp. The swamp just happened to be full of cannibals who were really good with blow darts, which was a bit of bad luck, really, and so he had to keep dodging them, too. Well, the son accidentally..."

"Lucy, this is a sock in a biscuit barrel," said Pandora, getting exasperated, "not a man-eating shark. There are no active volcanoes or dart-blowing cannibals this side of Potters Bar, as far as I know, so we needn't worry about them. The doctor's surgery is only on the High Street. And I'm not asking you to hold its mouth to stop it eating my leg, just sit on the lid while I tidy this mess. So, please be quiet and do it!"

Lucy sat down obediently, though she clearly wasn't at all happy about her part in the proceedings. She muttered things about bites and rashes and cream and injections all the time Pandora put the packets back into the cupboards and cleared up the mess in front of the fridge. She was still chuntering about spots and itches in embarrassing places as Pandora finally gathered up the biscuits from the floor and put them inside a plastic carrier bag, stuffing the whole lot in the cupboard under the sink.

Pandora had just finished when her dad walked into the kitchen. He had taken off his shirt while he was upstairs packing, because it was hot and sticky work, meaning his stomach was in full and glorious view. Pandora wished the ground would swallow her up. His stomach, though not quite the same size as Pandora's mum's, was nonetheless still impressive. It hung lazily over the belt of his work trousers like it needed a rest. Pandora had never once seen Lucy's dad's stomach. It was always tucked neatly inside his shirt, out of the way. Lucy had now been confronted with both her parents' stomachs, and in one day. It was all getting a bit too much for Pandora.

"We've got a chair if you'd rather," he said to Lucy, pointing at the biscuit barrel. "I generally find they are more comfortable to sit on."

"Thank you, Mr. Johnson," said Lucy politely, "but we are playing a game. It's my turn to sit on the biscuit barrel while Pandora finds the key I've hidden. It's a game called, 'Find the Hidden Key While the Other Person Sits on the Biscuit Barrel'. Did you never play it at school? We play it all the time. It's one of our favourites."

Inside, Pandora groaned. It sounded so lame, though it was pretty good for Lucy.

"No, football was more my game," said Pandora's dad, sweeping his foot through the air as if he were taking a free kick. "They used to call me the George Best of Alderman Barnett High School for Boys."

Lucy had absolutely no idea who he was talking about but smiled sweetly anyway.

"But, that was then and this is now," he continued wistfully. "I didn't come down to talk about my footballing days. Pandora, where did I put those new rolls of sticky tape?"

Pandora quickly fished one out of the drawer near the washing machine. "Here's one," she said with forced cheeriness. "Now you can go back upstairs and get on."

"Getting rid of me, are you?" said her dad, smiling. "It must be a good game if you don't want to play it in front of me. Must be something secret, eh?"

"Very," said Pandora truthfully. "See you later."

With that, and whistling 'Rockin' all over the World' almost in tune, Pandora's dad went back upstairs to his packing.

"Well done, Lucy!" congratulated Pandora. "You completely fooled him: though how he bought such a pathetic story I will never know."

"Thank you," replied Lucy preening herself at her quick thinking. "You aren't the only one around here with brains, Pandora.

"But I'm not sitting here for much longer," she continued. "I can feel the sock moving around inside and I don't like it one bit. I think it is very angry at being caught. What are we going to do with it? I can't walk round with a biscuit barrel attached to my bottom forever. I mean, there's Auntie Pam's barbecue to get ready for. Mum will notice the bulge under my dress. And I won't be able to sit on any of the garden chairs."

"We'll take it down to the shed," answered Pandora. "Once inside we'll seal the lid tight with some of Dad's sticky tape. We'll put the socks back into the drawer at the same time, when they are all caught. That way we don't have to open the drawer more than once."

"Good idea," agreed Lucy. She was happy with any suggestion that would quickly separate her bottom from the lid.

Pandora grabbed a roll of sticky tape while Lucy stood up carefully. The biscuit barrel was pressed tight against her bottom. Pandora opened the kitchen door and followed Lucy out. Lucy waddled like a duck towards the shed. Once safely inside, and with the door shut securely, the girls sealed the lid. At Lucy's insistence Pandora used up the whole roll. Lucy was adamant they made small air holes in the lid for the sock to breath. Pandora wasn't sure this was necessary what with the sock being, after all, a sock, and having lived in the drawer for some time. But Lucy had sat on the lid and Pandora knew it as only fair to take note. Miss Watkins always said that when you worked in pairs you had to listen to your partner and value their opinions.

"Well, we know one thing," said Pandora, as the girls opened the door of the shed and stepped out onto the garden path, "If this one is anything to go by they don't seem to have strayed too far. We might be in luck."

"You're right about that, Pandora," cried Lucy, pointing over the garden fence. "Look!"

In Mrs Dunstan's garden, next door but two, the red sock was wiggling slowly along the washing line. As it slid along it was pulling off the pegs one by one. Mrs Dunstan's clean washing was falling gently onto the lawn like the first leaves of autumn.

"Quickly, Lucy!" shouted Pandora, stealing a glance back inside the shed. "Grab that fishing net and follow me!"

11

The girls dashed out of the gate like horses released from their traps. They darted along the narrow alleyway that lay like a neatly ploughed furrow between the rear gardens of the rows of terraced houses. It was only a few leaps and bounds to Mrs Dunstan's gate and the girls reached it in seconds. Like Pandora's gate, it was always left on the latch. Pandora and Lucy hurried inside her garden, and then froze, horror-struck at the awful sight before them.

Mrs Dunstan's washing lay like a thin multi-coloured carpet across her tidy green lawn. Above it was an empty washing line, swaying uselessly between two painted posts in the light summer breeze. Scattered around the washing were the pegs, lying exactly where they fell like soldiers after a battle.

Although she was a widow and lived on her own, Mrs Dunstan always had a full line of sparkling washing. Pandora's mum did as little cleaning and tidying as possible, even when she wasn't pregnant. Mrs Dunstan, however, was very house-proud. She spent most of her waking hours happily dusting, vacuuming and washing, or bathing and combing Honeysuckle. Pandora knew she would be devastated to find her washing scattered around like this.

At the far end of the washing line a huge red sock sat smirking at the girls. From his mouth sparkled a pair of Mrs. Dunstan's gigantic white knickers, the sort with long legs you normally see only in pantomimes or adverts in Gentle Ladies' Magazines. The sock had tied a thick knot in the end of each of the legs.

As the girls watched, the sock slid off the line and, using the knickers for a parachute, floated gracefully to the ground. Then, like a jack in a box, he slithered back up the line post, and drifted down once more. The sock was clearly intent on enjoying itself.

"Stop that!" screamed Pandora. She was fuming. "Mrs. Dunstan is really nice. She's done nothing to you, so you shouldn't be doing anything to her, and especially not to her knickers. It's not polite. Come here at once, and help us tidy this mess up."

But the sock had no intention whatsoever of obeying Pandora. Instead, he dropped the knickers from his mouth just long enough to let his liquorice coloured tongue slowly stick out in defiance, before picking up the knickers and slinking up the pole once more.

"That's it!" cried Pandora, absolutely livid. She was angrier even than the time Charlie Springer had told the supply teacher a lie about Pandora, saying she had put a test tube full of hairy caterpillars down the back of Natalie Williams' vest, when it was him all the time, and Pandora had been told to sit quietly in the Thinking Corner - the only time ever - for the rest of the science lesson. "You're for it now! Come on, Lucy. Bring that net!"

Pandora and Lucy, fishing net in hand, shot up the garden path towards the sock. At the same moment, the sock flung itself off the line for another parachute ride down to earth.

The girls reached the sock as the sock reached the ground. Lucy thrust the net towards the sock like a collector chasing a butterfly. She missed by a tiny fraction. Instead she scooped up Mrs. Dunstan's colossal knickers. Deprived of his parachute, the sock slinked swiftly across Mrs. Dunstan's perfectly groomed lawn, straight towards her beautiful flower border. The girls followed on behind.

"Missed me, missed me!" taunted the sock in a deep bass voice as it slid into the border. It slid in and out of the bushes and plants Mrs. Dunstan had grown so lovingly over the years. As it went back and forth the sock flicked its tail up and down like a whip, deliberately knocking the heads off the flowers and plants one by one.

Pandora and Lucy tracked the sock through the border like hunters after their prey. Lucy was poised with the net high in the air waiting for the moment when the sock emerged. Although it was obvious where the sock was from the swishing movements amongst the plants and bushes, Lucy didn't want to bring the net down into the flower border in case she missed the sock and knocked off even more flower heads in the process.

"It's not coming out, Pandora!" shouted Lucy after a few tense moments. "The flowers are getting ruined. What shall we do?"

"Stay here," ordered Pandora. She rushed across the lawn towards Mrs Dunstan's back door. "I've got a better idea."

By Mrs Dunstan's back door was an outside tap. On it hung an old gunmetal watering can. Mrs Dunstan used it for watering her plants and filling up her birdbath. Pandora filled the watering can to the brim. Then she ran back to where Lucy was standing guard.

"Where is it?" asked Pandora, casting her eye rapidly over the flowerbed.

"Inside the bush with the little blue flowers," replied Lucy, pointing at the spot. "You can see it rustling the leaves. Quick, Pandora! Do something before it knocks off all the heads!"

Pandora took the filter off the spout, so that the water would gush out like a torrent rather than in a drizzle of fine rain. She lifted the watering can high over the place Lucy had indicated and took aim. Without hesitation, she tipped the can forward sharply. Water surged out of the spout and, within seconds, drenched the bush and its surroundings completely.

When the watering can was empty Pandora flung it behind her onto the lawn. She knelt down and, thrusting her hands into the flowerbed, prized apart the bush.

"Be careful, Pandora," shouted Lucy, taking a step back. "It might jump up and bite you!"

"Not now, Lucy," said Pandora confidently. "Look."

Lucy peered into the space made by Pandora's outstretched hands. The red sock was lying pathetically on the ground. It was completely still. Its tongue was dangling lamely from its crumpled mouth. It was totally sodden.

"It's too heavy to move now, Lucy," explained Pandora jubilantly. "It may be an unusual sock, but it is still made of wool. It has absorbed a great deal of water. It won't be able to cause us any more trouble until it is dried out.

"Though, on a hot day like this, that won't take long," she continued. Pandora knew all about evaporation, having beaten Pollyanna

Pritchard by one mark in a recent science test on the water cycle. "We'd better move fast."

Between them Pandora and Lucy gathered up the squidgey sock. Lucy insisted on taking the tail end, reminding Pandora that she mustn't be bitten before Auntie Pam's barbecue. They dumped their soggy cargo into the watering can. Together they carried the can across the garden to the outside tap. Pandora turned on the tap while Lucy held the watering can in place.

"It can't escape if it stays wet," explained Pandora. "So we'll keep it soaked in water."

"But what if it can't swim?" asked Lucy as the water began to rise. "I don't want it to drown, Pandora, however horrid it has been."

Pandora quickly explained that it couldn't drown, what with it being a sock. However, at Lucy's insistence, and though it made no difference at all, Pandora agreed to only fill the can about three-quarters full, just in case.

"Dad said Mrs Dunstan was going for her grandchildren," observed Pandora, turning the tap off and drying her hands down the front of her yellow t-shirt. "That should give us enough time to tidy up the washing before she returns."

"What about the flowers, Pandora?" asked Lucy. "Do you think she'll notice the damage?"

"I hope not," replied Pandora. "All we can do is pick up as many as of the broken heads as we can and hide them in our recycle bin at home. We'll just have to hope the gaps aren't too obvious."

Pandora began to peg the washing back on the line. By working steadily along the trail of clothes and hanging them directly above their landing place Pandora assumed she was returning them in the same order they had dropped to the ground. The one thing she did not know was from which part of the line Mrs Dunstan's knickers had originally been hanging, as these had been in the sock's mouth and could have come from anywhere. She presumed, however, that an elderly lady like Mrs Dunstan wouldn't want anyone and everyone to see her underwear blowing cheerfully in the wind. She guessed they had been closest to the house and, therefore, furthest from the alleyway. With something of a struggle, for the sock had been good at knots, Pandora untied the legs and hung the knickers at the kitchen end of the line, immediately next to the post.

Lucy, meanwhile, gathered up the broken flower heads and put them into the fishing net. When she had collected them all she stepped back to examine the border. Lucy was greatly relieved to see that nothing appeared to be too obviously damaged. The only thing that appeared odd was that one bush was shiny and wet on what was otherwise a blazingly hot, sunny day. Lucy crossed her fingers and arms, turned around and touched her nose like Pandora had done in the shed. She hoped it would mean that by the time Mrs Dunstan came home to show her grandchildren Honeysuckle's new puppies, both the bush and the ground around it would once more be bone dry.

"Well done, Lucy," declared Pandora, as she joined her friend by the flowerbed. "It doesn't look as if the sock was able to do too much harm, after all."

"What are we going to do with the sock?' asked Lucy. "We can't borrow Mrs Dunstan watering can for long. She'll notice if it's missing."

"I'll nip home and get Dad's watering can instead," replied Pandora. "We'll transfer it from one to the other. It'll be perfectly safe in there. You stay here and watch the sock until I get back."

Pandora ran back to her dad's shed. While she was there she took a minute to check on the biscuit barrel. It was still sealed tight. From within an angry slithering sound could be heard. Content that the blue sock remained secure Pandora returned to Lucy. She had in her hand her dad's plastic green watering can. It was the cheapest sort the garden centre sold. It looked rubbish beside Mrs. Dunstan's smart metal can.

This time Pandora held her dad's watering can under the tap while Lucy turned it on. Repeating her earlier worry about the sock drowning, whatever Pandora said, Lucy filled it only about three quarters full of water. The girls then slipped the squelchy sock out of Mrs Dunstan's watering can and plopped it into the green plastic one. The sock was limp and squashy, like an utterly exhausted eel, and was certainly going to cause nobody any trouble whilst it was in its present condition.

Pandora emptied Mrs Dunstan's watering can down the drain. She hung it back in precisely the same place she had found it. The girls then carried the full watering can down the garden and out into the alleyway. They closed Mrs Dunstan's gate behind them.

Furtively they stole a glance around them. No one else was in the alleyway. No one was peering at them from any of the windows that overlooked Mrs Dunstan's garden. It appeared the girls had remained totally unseen.

"Phew, that was close!" breathed out Pandora, relaxing for a moment. "I think we've got away with it. Let's get this one back to the shed."

They carried the watering can as carefully as they could along the alleyway. A few slops of water sloshed out as they walked the few short steps back to Pandora's garden. Once safely inside the gate they opened the shed door and deposited the watering can beside the biscuit barrel. Together they stood in the open doorway.

"How long do you think it will be before the water evaporates?" asked Lucy. She was anxious not to have to deal with either of the socks again. "I'm honestly not being funny, but it really is hot in your shed, Pandora."

"Ages," replied Pandora without hesitation. "Do you remember the science experiment a few weeks ago with the plastic bowl full of salty water? The one Miss Watkins had on the windowsill? That took days to evaporate, though I'm convinced Tommy Randall poured water in on more than one occasion when Miss Watkins wasn't looking. We've got hours before we need to worry about this amount drying out, even in a hot shed."

The girls closed and bolted the shed door. They wandered slowly up the path towards Pandora's house. Although they had caught two of the socks, neither of the girls felt like celebrating. That could wait until all three were safely back inside the drawer. Further, though their stomachs told them it must be getting near lunchtime, neither felt terribly much like eating. That could wait until later, too.

"Where on earth can the green one be?" mused Pandora, more to herself than to Lucy. "It is obviously the leader of the gang. It is bound to be the trickiest to catch. But if the other two have stayed so close, then their leader can't have wandered too far. They must have planned to stick together."

As if in reply, a familiar sound began to echo along the otherwise quiet terrace. Pandora pricked up her ears, suddenly alert. In the distance, it sounded as if Tam was barking madly at the front window of Mr. Mower's house.

Pandora knew instantly something must be wrong. Because it was Saturday lunchtime and Tam never barked then. Mr. Mower wouldn't be loading his van until Monday. He was out for a pub lunch with Mrs Mower, like they always did on a Saturday, before they walked to the market for the weekend's fruit and vegetables. Something else must have vexed Tam for him to be barking like this. In an instant Pandora thought she knew exactly what it might be.

12

As the girls flew through the back door of Pandora's house they discovered Pandora's mum rifling the kitchen cupboards. She was wearing a puzzled look.

"Have you seen the biscuit barrel, Pandora?" she asked. "Dad said he had got me some of those yummy chocolate thingummies. I can't find the biscuit barrel anywhere and I'm starving. It seems like forever since I had those jam tarts.

"Got to keep feeding Charlie, you know," she added, patting her tummy, as if this was a perfectly good excuse for permanently stuffing herself with anything she could lay her hands on. "Eating for two is hard work."

"Dad put the biscuits in the cupboard under the sink," replied Pandora, trying desperately to squeeze past her mum and out of the house through the front door. This was the quickest way to the street and the answer to why Tam was barking so frantically. Her mum, however, was too big and fat to make passing in the kitchen an easy or speedy manoeuvre. "I think you'll find them in a carrier bag."

"What a ridiculous place to put them," said Pandora's mum, squatting down and opening the cupboard door, a movement that pulled her t-shirt even further up over her bump. "This is where we keep the cleaning stuff. He knows we don't put food in there. What on earth made him do that?"

"I suspect he was in a hurry to get back to his packing, Mrs Johnson," suggested Lucy. "He probably didn't think and put them in there by mistake with the washing up liquid. My dad is always putting things in the wrong place. Once he put the goldfish food into the freezer along with the ice cream. It took us ages to find it. My mum was really cross, as one of the goldfish died of starvation whilst we were hunting for it and they had to buy me another one."

"Possibly," agreed Pandora's mum uncertainly. "But he has always put things away properly before. It's me who is the disorganised one in this house.

"Ah! This looks like it," she said eventually. She peered inside the carrier bag. "It's strange of him not to use the biscuit barrel. And lots of the biscuits seem broken."

"They were cheaper that way," said Pandora. She felt guilty at lying but it was crucial she got past Mum and out to Tam without delay. "In fact, I'm sure Dad said they were doing a special offer on broken biscuits at the supermarket."

"Oh well," mumbled Pandora's mum, popping a broken chocolate cookie into her mouth. "They still taste good." She began to chew happily.

"Why don't you take them all through to the living room?" suggested Pandora, seizing the moment. She guided her mum out of the kitchen. "Sit down and have as many as you want. Charlie must be hungry. And you must be very tired."

"Thank you, Pandora," said Pandora's mum through a mouthful of cookie. She was touched by Pandora's sudden and most unusual show of concern. "I suppose you're right. It's exhausting being pregnant you know, having to sit around all the time, watching the TV and eating. It's so nice that you understand."

Pandora led her mum back to the chair in front of the TV. Once she was settled and eating contentedly Pandora came out of the room. She closed the door firmly behind her.

"Come on, Lucy," she whispered urgently. "Let's go and see what Tam is making such a noise about."

The girls scampered through the front door and down the short paved path. Attached to the low metal gate, rusted at the hinges, was an estate agent's sign. Written boldly across it was the word 'SOLD'. They were through the gate in seconds.

At the gate they turned sharp right and sprinted to the end of the terrace to where Mr. and Mrs Mower lived. Once outside the house they looked through the front window. Tam was wagging his tail like crazy. He was also jumping against the window from his watchtower on the settee.

After a quick glance up and down the street, which was utterly deserted, Pandora told Lucy that Tam must have got himself worked up over something to do with Mr. Mower's van. It was the only thing he ever got this excited about. Also, as Tam was barking out of the front window, Pandora said that whatever was concerning him was clearly not inside the house.

At Pandora's instruction, she and Lucy sprinted quickly around the van. From a quick inspection of the outside, however, it wasn't easy to see why Tam was in such an excited state. The doors were all closed.

Pandora tried the handles and all were firmly locked. The tyres looked fine. No one seemed to have interfered with the paintwork or wing mirrors in any way. There appeared to be little reason for Tam to be so stressed out.

"Perhaps it has nothing to do with the van, after all," suggested Lucy. "It might have been the milk float. Tam might have been upset by the funny whirring sound the battery makes. He might be worried we are being invaded by Zongoids or something. It's what I always think when I hear a milk float."

"Why's that?" asked Pandora, totally baffled.

"Because I once saw this film, *'They Came from Planet Zong'*," Lucy explained. "A group of aliens, who looked like a cross between a newt and a squirrel, crash-landed in a disued quarry. They had come to earth to find a Zongoid Princess called Gongolina who had been kidnapped by the evil Lord Frong and hidden in a cave. She was heir to the Zongoid throne, and Lord Frong wanted her out of the way so he could rule Zong instead. It was his ambition to be the big boss of Zong.

"Anyway these aliens, who were loyal to the true Zongoid royal family, and who had vowed to die rather than return without her, found Princess Gongolina in the cave, because she wore a special bracelet that beeped out a sort of Zongoid SOS. They had to get her back home to Zong before Lord Frong - who had meanwhile become Prime Minister of Great Britain and was using his evil powers to suck the mind juices out of all the politicians and world leaders, so he would have loads of ideas about how to rule Zong - realised that she had been rescued. But the crash had ruined their engine, and so they had to build a new one. Just before Lord Frong captured them using the American air force, which he was now in charge of because he had also sucked out the mind juices of the President, they managed to escape. They used the battery from a milk float as their power source. The bit when they took off just in time was really exciting. They even took a few yoghurts home with them, but I think that was for experiments because all they ate were cucumbers normally.

"It was a great film," she concluded. "Though there was this really sad bit about the milkman. He lost his job because he couldn't get to work in the morning without the battery, and the milk float was too heavy for him to push by himself back to the depot. No one would believe him when he phoned up and said that he had been chained up by aliens who only spoke Zong - which, of course, he couldn't understand properly because he only did French at school - and who looked like newty squirrels wearing tin foil."

"Thank you, Lucy," said Pandora dryly. "But it can't have been a passing milk float that made Tam bark. It's almost lunchtime. The milkmen will all be back home by now. They will have finished their rounds hours ago. The only time I have ever heard Tam keep on barking like this is when it has something to do with Mr. Mower's van."

Pandora and Lucy looked towards Mr. and Mrs Mower's house. Tam continued to bark uncontrollably in the front window.

"He's making a real racket, Lucy,' said Pandora. "We don't seem to have reassured him by looking round the van. I think I'll check it over one more time.

Pandora started at the front. Placing her hands over her eyes to keep out the glare of the sun, she looked first into the cabin through the side window nearest the steering wheel. It appeared no different from when she and her dad had ridden in it to Mr. Brewster's Furniture Emporium a little earlier. She couldn't see through to the back of the van, however, because Mr. Mower had inserted a huge piece of plywood behind the seats some years before. It separated the cabin from the rear cargo area and stopped people seeing whether there was anything on board that could be pinched.

Pandora worked her way slowly down the driver's side of the vehicle, rubbing her hands underneath the doors and side, and especially inside the wheel arches. Nothing appeared to be out of the ordinary. She reached the rear doors, where she again tried the handles. They remained firmly locked together. Although these doors each had a small observation window Mr. Mower had also covered them on the inside with two further pieces of plywood.

Pandora returned back down the passenger side of the van, feeling her way methodically along the underneath as she went. It wasn't long before she was back where she had started. Her examination had revealed nothing unusual. Tam appeared to gain no reassurance from the inspection, however. He was still barking as vigorously as he had been doing since before the girls arrived.

"There's nothing wrong with the outside, Lucy," said Pandora. She was thoroughly puzzled. "Nor does it look like it's been broken into. I simply can't imagine why Tam is making such a fuss."

"I can, Pandora," cried Lucy. The colour drained away from her face in an instant. She pointed to the roof of the van. "Look up there!"

While Pandora had checked over the van Lucy had remained on the pavement. In fact, she had taken a step or two back from the road. Mindful of Auntie Pam's barbecue that evening, and fearful of her mum's anger at any bruise, blemish or blot that she might pick up, Lucy had put a little distance between herself and anything that might jump out of the van and bash her. As well as giving her some protection, this position had also given her a good view of the van as a whole, including the little whirly air vent on the roof that spun around as the van drove along.

It was towards this vent that Lucy was now pointing. During the latter part of Pandora's examination it had begun mysteriously to spin round at great speed, even though presently there was no breeze at all. Then it had stopped as abruptly as it had started. As Lucy watched, a thin black tongue had emerged through the air vent, licking the air as if sensing who was around. The tongue had quickly been followed by a pair of stony black eyes, set in a woollen face of the brightest of emerald greens.

'The last sock!" cried Lucy, her finger as still as a church weather vane in the serene, sleepy air. "It must have crawled through the air vent and got inside Mr. Mower's van. That's why Tam is going mad! Oh, Pandora, what are we going to do?"

"That is a very good question for one who appears to be so stupid," sneered the sock. "Just what *are* you going to do? Crawl through here and join me?" The sock laughed a hollow, creepy laugh. "I don't think so, do you? I think you'll just have to let me get on with my little plan. Actually, I hoped that awful yapping dog would bring you running.

Artists should always have someone to admire their work. That's why I've waited for you to join me before I start."

With that, the sock slid back inside the vent. For a moment neither girl could move or do anything. They were paralysed with fear, as rigid as the statues outside the Town Hall. They were at a complete loss what to do. Getting into Pandora's kitchen and Mrs Dunstan's garden was one thing. Getting into Mr. Mower's locked van was quite another.

From inside the van the girls heard a metal tool box being opened. This was followed by a high-speed whirring noise.

"Oh no!" yelled Pandora. She recognised the sound instantly. It was Mr. Mower's cordless drill. Her dad had one like it at home.

"Oh yes!" answered the sock.

The sock poked his face through the air vent once more.

"In case you're wondering, I'm going to drill lots of little holes into the sides of this van," it taunted maliciously. "Together they will spell the words, 'Blame Pandora'. That is your name, isn't it? I want everyone to know who to thank for letting me out. I think I've got plenty of time to write that out before you find a way of getting into this van.

"Here's a thought," it added nastily "Why not try Lucy's special box? After all, you said there are plenty of keys in there. Perhaps one will fit the van. You must be so glad by now you found the right one to open the drawer."

With a dreadful chuckle the sock slithered back inside the van. For a minute or two Pandora was dumbstruck. The prospect of what the sock was going to do was terrible. She imagined the shrill sound that would soon be scratching its eager way through the air. She saw in her mind's eye the sharp point of a drill bit repeatedly poking its way through the thin metal panel of the van. She pictured her name slowly being formed on the side. She had to stop the sock!

"The sock must never use that drill, Lucy," cried Pandora, shaking the ghastly nightmare out of her head. "It won't take the sock long to ruin Mr. Mower's van once it's worked out how to put the drill bit together. Who knows what else it might decide to write!"

"But what can we do to stop it?" asked Lucy bewildered. "None of my Gran's keys will fit the locks. They are much too old to be of use. There's nothing else for it, Pandora. We'll have to get your dad."

Pandora was about to agree. There seemed to be no other solution. Dad would have to be told everything. Then she looked back towards Mr. and Mrs Mower's house. Tam was still jumping up and down at the window like a supercharged Jack-in-a-Box. As Pandora looked at Tam a thought suddenly struck her. At the same time her hand strayed to her pocket.

"Wait a moment. Lucy," she said. "I've just had an idea!"

13

Pandora thrust her hand into her pocket. She pulled out her handkerchief. Unwrapping it carefully, Pandora stared long and hard at the last key inside.

"I've already told you the keys won't open the van!" complained Lucy. "They're far too old. They are also completely the wrong shape. This is a ridiculous idea, Pandora."

"I'm not thinking of opening the van with it," replied Pandora. "Listen for a moment, will you! Mr. and Mrs Mower's house has got the original front door from when the terrace was built in Victorian times. It's the only one in the row that is original, so it's a bit of a thing with them. Mr. and Mrs Mower are very proud of the door and have looked after it really carefully. It still has the original lock and it works like new. There is a chance, Lucy, that this key might open the lock. It must be about the same age. If we can get into the house we might be able to find the keys to Mr. Mower's van. That way we can open the van and capture that sock."

Lucy nodded her head in agreement. One matter troubled her, though.

"What about Tam?" she said, glancing nervously at the window. "Won't he bite us? I know he's friendly and all that when he is out on a lead with Mr. or Mrs Mower. But won't he think we are breaking into his house? He might be specially trained to bite burglars really hard on the ankles, or somewhere even more painful, and hold them fast in his jaws until the police arrive.

"Dogs can be specially trained to do all sorts of things, Pandora, and Tam has really sharp teeth. From here they look just like crocodile's teeth. And crocodiles can cut through speedboats and everything. My dad told me about a story from the newspaper where a man caught this crocodile and they cut it open and found a whole suit of armour inside its stomach. The newspaper couldn't say where the suit of armour had come from, because no one had reporting one missing, so it must have come from a shipwreck under the sea rather than from a castle, which the crocodile couldn't have got into anyway, being a crocodile. What I mean is they can eat almost anything with their teeth. Tam might be just the same.

Lucy slowed down and spoke almost in a whisper. "I don't ever want to be bitten again, Pandora. Not after last time. That was terrible."

Pandora knew immediately what Lucy meant. Lucy had looked after their class hamster, Cedric, during the last half-term holiday. Early on the first Saturday morning it had bitten her on the finger whilst she was changing the water bottle. Lucy, who could be clumsy on occasions, had accidentally prodded Cedric in the ribs with the drinking tube as she was pulling it out. Cedric had swivelled round and taken a nasty chunk out of her. Though as Lucy herself admitted at the first News Time after the holiday, really Cedric was only acting in self-defence.

Lucy's finger had swollen very badly over the next few hours. It became extremely painful. By the afternoon it was so bad that her dad had taken her to the Accident and Emergency Department of the hospital. Apart from Lucy, it was full of people who had got serious sporting injuries: rugby players with broken noses and fractured legs, footballers with dislocated ankles, and the like. Lucy was the only person in the hospital that day - possibly ever - suffering from injuries sustained during a hamster attack. One ghastly little boy with his arm in a sling after falling from his skateboard had even smirked really loudly when he heard Lucy's dad check her in at the reception desk. Not only had Lucy been in dreadful pain but also she had felt completely embarrassed.

A kindly nurse in a blue uniform with a crinkly white plastic apron and funny rubber gloves had given her an injection against something called tetanus. Lucy was still convinced tetanus was a hamster disease, one that made you sleep all day and then run around in a wheel all night. Lucy's finger had been put in a bandage and she hadn't been able to go swimming all week.

Pandora understood Lucy's fears. She knew Lucy wouldn't want to have to go to the hospital again and have another injection. Particularly as Lucy would be worried this time about catching dog diseases, ones where you might end up chasing sticks and going to the toilet in the park with everyone watching.

"He'll be really friendly, Lucy," Pandora reassured her. "He always licks me and makes a fuss when he sees me. I'm sure he knows we are trying to help. He'll be on our side. Trust me."

With a quick squeeze of Lucy's hand Pandora looked once more at the key. She studied it carefully and made her decision. She grabbed hold of Lucy and together the girls ran towards Mr. and Mrs Mower's front door.

"Here goes," said Pandora. She slipped the key into the lock. Tam immediately stopped barking and jumping up and down. It was as if he wanted to show them he knew what they were doing and was on their side. Instead, Tam wagged his tail from side to side so fast it looked like he might take off into the air at any moment.

The key slid straight into the lock without any struggle whatsoever. It clearly fitted, but would it open the door? Lucy crossed her arms, legs and fingers like mad and swivelled around twice, becoming dizzy and nearly falling over in the process. Pandora turned the key sharply to the right. The key went round in a complete circle. The lock fell away instantly.

With the swiftest of triumphant glances the girls pushed down on the handle. Inside the thin, floral decorated hallway they were met by Tam. He bounced up to them and greeted them like they were his very best friends in the whole world. Lucy, scared that this friendliness was all a sham and that Tam was going to take a bite out of her at any moment, stood behind Pandora for protection. Tam, meanwhile, danced a merry jig around them both.

"We've no time for this Tam," said Pandora, stroking him and attempting to calm him down. "We need the keys to the van. Where are they, boy? Can you help us?"

As if to show them that, of course, he would help, and that only the stupidest dog in the universe would not know where it's owner's van keys were, Tam bounded down the narrow hallway to a coat stand at the bottom of the stairs. Barking like he had never barked before, Tam sprang up and down on his little back legs thrusting himself high into the air. At the height of each leap Tam nuzzled the pocket of an old checked coat that was hanging closest to the wall.

"Mr. Mower's work jacket," cried Pandora, recognising it instantly. "Of course! The keys to the van must be in there!"

Quick as a flash Pandora grabbed the jacket off the stand, and shoved her hand into the pocket. Amongst the sweet wrappers, screws and tissues - some of which were sticky and soggy - she found a bunch of keys. She recognised them as the same bunch her dad had used to drive the van earlier.

"Well done, Tam!" congratulated Pandora. Tam barked happily in reply.

Pandora threw the jacket onto the stairs. Holding the keys aloft like she was an Olympic runner carrying the torch to the opening ceremony, Pandora rushed out of the front door. Lucy followed on close behind. Not to be outdone, Tam scampered after them both, barking and yelping as he went.

They arrived at the van to find that the sock had not yet started drilling. However, from the noises coming from inside of metal being tightened against metal, as if the last few turns to fix the drill bit in place were being completed, it was obvious it wouldn't be long in coming.

At the sound of Tam's barking the sock appeared once more at the vent. Pandora immediately hid the keys behind her back. It was vital the sock did not know they now had a way of getting into the van. Otherwise it might decide to escape through the vent and shoot off into the distance. There would never be a chance like this to capture it again.

"Oh, there you are," scoffed the sock. "I'm just about ready. I've had a bit of trouble tightening the mouth of the drill - it's rather difficult when you have no hands. But I'm nearly there. A few more turns and the fun can start. Let me see. It is P.A.N.D.O.R.A., isn't it?"

With a wicked laugh the sock slipped back through the vent. The sound of metal being tightened could be heard once more.

"What do we do now, Pandora?" whispered Lucy. "I know we've got the key and all that. But remember what happened at the shed. That sock packs a nasty punch. What are we going to do once we've opened the doors?"

Pandora stood perfectly still for a moment. Up to now she hadn't thought about this part. All she had focussed on was getting hold of the keys.

"Give me a moment Lucy," Pandora replied. She closed her eyes. As she did so a brilliantly simple plan popped straight into her head. When she had run through it twice in her mind to make sure there were no obvious flaws, she opened her eyes and looked directly at Lucy.

"This is what we're going to do," began Pandora, and she whispered her plan into Lucy's waiting ear.

14

Lucy stood ready and in position. She looked like a boxer in a ring waiting for the bell to signal the start of the first round. Her right arm was outstretched and looked as if it was poised to give a perfect jab to the nose. Her other hand, appeared ready for a neat uppercut to her opponent's chin. In fact, one of Lucy's hands was gripping the key to the rear door, a key inserted carefully and quietly so as not to disturb the sock inside, whilst the other grasped the shiny handle.

Pandora was standing next to Lucy, though half a pace behind her. Her legs were astride. She was holding Tam in her arms like a rugby player ready to pass the ball.

Pandora's plan was beautifully simple and uncomplicated, like the best plans always are. Pandora had whispered to Lucy that, on her signal, Lucy should twist the key and open the door as speedily and as noiselessly as she could: the element of surprise was crucial. As the door flew open Pandora would hurl Tam into the back of the van in the general direction of the sock. The door would then be slammed shut while Tam dealt with the sock. Once the sock had been overcome, the girls would open the door and escort the bruised and battered sock back to Pandora's shed.

Lucy thought it sounded perfect, though she had expressed one concern.

"But what if the sock gets the better of Tam?" she had whispered apprehensively. "It's really violent, Pandora. Look at what it did to your eye. What if Tam isn't up to the job? We both know he can bark like there is no tomorrow, but can he fight? We don't want to have to explain a damaged van and a dazed dog to Mr. and Mrs Mower, Pandora. That might be a bit much for them."

"Don't worry, Lucy," Pandora had responded confidently, "Mr. Mower has told me lots of times that Scottie's were originally bred in Scotland to hunt haggises. From what he told me about haggises they sound really fierce, though I always thought they were sheep's bladders filled with meat and stuff. But Mr. Mower should know. After all, he and Mrs Mower have been on a coach tour to the Isle of Skye. Dangerous socks should be easy compared to haggises. Tam will be fine."

The reassurance had settled Lucy. She had got into position and taken her stance.

With Lucy at the ready, Pandora had picked up Tam. Tam had showed his enthusiasm for Pandora's plan by nudging her face repeatedly, his wet nose leaving a silver trail on her freckly cheek. Then he had gone stiff and alert. His ears had shot upwards and his quivering nose had become like a radar scanner sensing the enemy's position.

With all three thus prepared, Pandora began counting. "One, two, three," she mouthed to Lucy.

At the count of three, Lucy twisted the key and turned the handle. As the rear door swung open, a shaft of gilded sunlight streaked into the van. The burst of sudden brightness was brilliantly intense, scattering before it the gloom of the blackened van. For a few precious moments the sock was completely blinded. Instinctively, the sock turned away from the light. In the process it dropped the drill from its mouth.

Taking aim with Tam - teeth bared, eyes fixed and paws at the ready - Pandora lost no time. She threw him towards the squinting sock. Tam flew through the air like a bleached version of a canine super hero. The girls had just enough time to see Tam make a perfect landing of the sock's head and neck and of the blinded sock buckling beneath Tam's paws. Then Lucy shut the door with a great slam and locked it once more.

Pandora and Lucy each glued an ear to one of the back doors of Mr. Mower's van. Together they listened whilst Tam set about his prey.

Within seconds of Tam's first grizzly growl it was all over. Tam's frisky yapping announced the result to the girls as clearly as if it had been flashed up onto a big screen.

"Wow! Haggises stood no chance!" exclaimed Lucy. She was deeply impressed at Tam's fighting spirit. "If Scotties can do that to such a nasty sock, it's no wonder they made mincemeat of haggises. It's amazing they didn't become totally extinct."

With a nod of agreement Pandora opened the rear door. Inside, Tam was sitting down on his haunches. There was not a scratch or mark to be seen anywhere on his snow-white body. The only clue Tam had done something energetic was that his little pink tongue was hanging out of his lightly panting mouth. His head was cocked to one side, in the familiar Scottie fashion. It made Tam look eager and uncertain at one and the same time, like he was waiting for further instructions.

Pinned beneath Tam's two fronts paws, lying as flat as a pancake, was the stunned sock. Its thin black tongue, dangling weakly from the sock's gawping mouth, looked no more deadly than an out of date liquorices bootlace. Its intense stony black eyes, the same eyes that earlier had stained Pandora and Lucy's souls with their inky darkness, appeared at that moment no more evil than a pair of half sucked chocolate raisins. The sock looked totally bewildered and beaten.

"Good boy, Tam!" shouted Pandora. "That was fantastic." She leant towards him and rubbed his head with her hand. Tam responded by swishing his tail enthusiastically across the floor of the van. It scattered bits of rubbish and sweet wrappers in the process. At the same time his tongue sprang back into life, covering her hand with slobbery silver licks.

"It serves you right," bellowed Lucy at the lifeless emerald stain under Tam's paws.

"You are a nasty, horrid creature! Do you know what we are going to do? We are going to lock you away forever. Then we are going to throw away the key. We will never speak to you again and neither of us is ever going to listen to a word you say."

Lucy flicked back her fringe, which had fallen over her eyes during her animated speech. It was a final, grand gesture of defiance against all things green and woollen.

"Well said, Lucy!" agreed Pandora, drying her sticky hand on her t-shirt. "That told him."

Pandora put her arms round Lucy. She felt a powerful mixture of triumph and relief at having caught the third sock. Lucy felt the same. The two girls gave each other the sort of hug that teammates give when they have just won a competition. As they unwrapped their arms, Pandora caught sight of her watch.

"Oh no!" cried Pandora in a sudden panic. "It's just gone one o'clock. My mum and dad will soon wonder where we are. I don't want them finding us out here with Tam and the sock and Mr. Mower's keys. They'll ask far too many questions. We'd better work fast."

"What do you want me to do?" asked Lucy hurriedly. She had suddenly caught Pandora's panic. She knew that if she didn't return home very soon to get washed, brushed, combed and dressed for Auntie Pam's barbecue, her mum would go mad and demand to know the reason for her lateness. "I'll do anything but sit on the sock. If there is any sitting to be done this time, it will be your turn. That will be fair."

"You tidy up the van, Lucy," instructed Pandora. "Then lock it, return the keys to Mr. Mower's jacket, hang it back on the stand and re-lock the front door with your granny's key. It shouldn't take you very long. It looks like the sock concentrated on the cordless drill and didn't take anything else out. There's only really the drill to put away.

"And by the look of the van, Lucy, Mr. Mower will never remember where the drill was originally." She peered around the messy and disorganised compartment. "As long as it is back in its box you can safely put it anywhere. You'd better scatter the sweet wrappers about a bit, too. Tam's tail has swept them up neatly to the sides."

"What are you going to do?" enquired Lucy.

"I'm going to take the sock back to the shed," replied Pandora.

"By yourself?" cried Lucy in disbelief. "That is so dangerous, Pandora. Are you sure? What if the sock comes round? Shouldn't you call the police or MI5 or someone? They will probably send marksmen in goggles and body armour to protect you. They might even call out helicopters and fighter planes to follow you round the terrace, especially if you tell them how the sock flicked you in the eye."

Within seconds Lucy was in full flow. "I saw this film once, Pandora, where this woman was left in a room to guard a mutant vampire bat that was supposed to be asleep. It had nested in her attic. Her house had once been the home of this mad professor who used to breed strange animals and birds, though the estate agents never told her anything about him or the animals when she bought the house. She only discovered the bat when she went into the attic after hearing some strange noises. Of course, she was a bit miffed at finding a mutant bat in there because she had only ever had house martins nesting near her gutters before.

"So she called one of the world's top experts in mutant vampire bats for help. He was called Doctor Von Rinkleburg. He came over from Transylvania where he lived in this creepy castle. He stunned the bat using a crossbow with an arrow that had been dipped in a special sleeping potion. Doctor Von Rinkleburg assured her the bat would lie perfectly still while he went to his car to fetch a special cage to put it in. However, the bat woke up while he was out of the room and..."

"Don't worry, Lucy," interrupted Pandora, sensing that this could be a long story. "I'm not going by myself. I'm going to take Tam. He can carry the sock for me in his mouth. It'll never escape from him."

Tam wagged his tail even more enthusiastically as if to show how happy he was with this proposal. More sweet papers were swept aside as a result. Tam would have barked, too, only now he had the sock trapped between his vice-like jaws.

"I'll wait for you at the shed," she continued. "You should only be a minute or two here. It's probably wisest to return the socks to the drawer all in one go. When they are safe we'll give Tam a chocolate biscuit as a reward, unless Mum has eaten them all. Finally, we'll take Tam back to Mr. and Mrs Mower's and go home for lunch."

"That's alright, then," said Lucy. She was more than happy with this suggestion. After all, there was no way the sock could do Pandora any harm if it was being guarded over by Tam.

With that Pandora beckoned Tam. He sprang obediently out of the van, sock in mouth, and trotted along the terrace behind Pandora. Lucy watched as Pandora took the long way round to the shed. Pandora didn't want to return through her house. Her mum might be causing a blockage and start asking awkward questions about why Pandora had in train both Tam and an emerald sock. Instead, she went along the full length of the street then disappeared down the alleyway beside the house at the far end of the terrace.

Once Tam and the sock were safely out of the way, for in truth she was more than a little nervous of both, Lucy set to work on the van. It took only a few minutes to replace the drill and the instruction booklet, and to scatter the sweet wrappers around. The sock had done no actual damage and, by the time Lucy had finished, there were absolutely no signs of any untoward activity.

Lucy locked the door and carried the keys back into the house. She put them back into Mr. Mower's jacket and hung it tidily back on the stand. Being a bit shorter than Pandora, however, she had to stand on the bottom step of the stairs and lean across to reach the peg. Lucy locked the front door with her granny's key. Finally, she closed the neat little garden gate that matched perfectly Mr. Mower's white-painted picket fence.

With a glance around her Lucy checked out the street. No one was around. The girls had once again remained totally unseen. It seemed as if, on this warm and balmy Saturday lunchtime, everyone was either being pregnant and resting, packing boxes, collecting grandchildren or having pub lunches. The street was eerily deserted. It was amazing, even a little weird. Out of the blue Lucy recalled a film where a whole town was abducted by aliens to be experimented on back on their planet. She wondered momentarily if the same thing had happened and that, for some reason, she had been left behind.

Lucy decided, however, that she and Pandora had just been very fortunate. With the happy conclusion that all was well and all manner of things were well, and that no aliens had abducted anybody, or at least not her, Lucy began to skip along the front of the terrace to rejoin her friend. A lightness of spirit filled Lucy.

By the time she reached the end of the terrace and was turning to go down the side of the end house, however, Lucy felt a heaviness descend once more. Two awful prospects lay before her, neither of which could be avoided. She still had to help Pandora put the socks back into the drawer. And, if that wasn't bad enough, she had to get ready for Auntie Pam's barbecue.

15

Stepping gingerly into the shed, for there was now even less room in there than earlier, Lucy found that Pandora had been busy.

The imprisoned socks were arranged in a neat line across what little space there was on the shed floor. Nearest the drawer was Dad's cheap plastic watering can. It had lost a good deal of water in the intense mid-day heat of the locked shed and was now about half full. In it, the red sock, soaked and sodden and much too heavy to escape, was struggling to make up its mind whether to float or sink. Next in line was the biscuit barrel. The barrel wobbled menacingly as the blue sock slithered around inside. Furthest from the drawer, and nearest the open door, Tam sat attentively on his haunches. Between his clenched teeth the emerald green sock dangled miserably.

Lucy noticed that, since she had last seen it, the green sock had become frayed around the neck. It looked to her as if it had caught on something sharp, like when the pocket of her school cardigan had got snagged on a nail sticking out of a neighbour's fence and she had made the snag into a huge tear when attempting to pull it free. Lucy asked what had happened.

Pandora explained that on the journey to the shed the green sock had repeatedly tried to escape, a foolishness that had been rewarded each time by a vigorous shake of Tam's head. As a result, a number of threads of wool had been pulled apart by Tam's sharp teeth. Pandora said the sock had eventually learned its lesson the hard way. Tattered and torn the emerald sock had finally given up trying to wriggle free. It now lay motionless with its head trapped firmly between Tam's jaws.

"As you can see, Lucy," said Pandora getting down to business, "we won't be able to have the door closed while we transfer the socks to the drawers. There simply won't be room for us to move if it is. I don't think this should matter, though. The socks will never be able to escape after what we're going to do to them."

Secretly, Lucy didn't mind having the door open one little bit. It meant there was no way she could get a nasty dose of heat rash in these final hours before Auntie Pam's barbecue. Wisely, however, she decided not to mention this fact to Pandora.

"Obviously we need to get the socks back into the drawer in the least dangerous order," continued Pandora, slipping seamlessly into teacher-mode. Lucy reflected silently that all Pandora needed at this moment was a pair of sensible spectacles and a navy cardigan that didn't quite fit and her final transformation into Miss Watkins would have been complete. "That is why they are lined up in the way they are. We will begin with the red sock. It is far too wet and heavy to move. You will place the watering can as near to the drawer as possible, while I lift the sock into the drawer using this net."

She held up a miniature fishing net. Pandora had once had two goldfish, called Samson and Delilah. Delilah had spent most of her short life chasing Samson round and round the bowl, while Samson had spent his life, until Delilah's mysterious and still unexplained death, trying to escape. Pandora had used the tiny net to transfer the goldfish to separate jam jars – times of sheer peace and joy to Samson

- while she cleaned out the bowl. Although the net itself was much too small to hold the sock, it could fit easily inside the mouth of the watering can. Pandora said she was going to hook the net under the sock, so she could lift it out without actually touching it.

"Won't the water stain the drawer, though, Pandora?" asked Lucy. Her dad had once stained their new oak-veneered coffee table by putting down his mug without using a mat. Though her dad had tried at first to cover his crime with a plant-pot, her mum had discovered it. She had gone berserk. The halo-like stain was now left exposed, except when visitors came and the plant pot was replaced, as a permanent reminder of his terrible misdeed and as a warning never to do the same again.

"Yes, it will," conceded Pandora. "But as it will be on the inside, and as I don't intend the drawer *ever* to be opened again, it doesn't really matter too much.

"We'll put the blue sock into the drawer next," she continued. "I'd like you to take the biscuit barrel, Lucy, and...

"I am not going to sit on the lid again if that is what you think!" interrupted Lucy. She had wondered if this might come up again. "No way, not ever." She folded her arms.

"I'm not going to ask you to do *that*, Lucy," responded Pandora irritably. "If you are sitting on the lid, how are we going to get the sock out?"

Lucy unfolded her arms sheepishly. Pandora had a point.

"If you will please listen for a moment, Lucy, you'll find out what to do," said Pandora. From her exasperated tone Lucy half expected her to add, "And if you interrupt again we'll never get out for lunch break."

"I want you to shake the biscuit barrel as hard as you can, until the sock has the biggest headache it has ever had," explained Pandora. "Then, when it doesn't know whether it is Monday or Tuesday..."

"But it is Saturday," remarked Lucy.

"Yes, I know it is,"' said Pandora. "What I mean is, when the sock is completely confused..."

"Well, just say that, then," pointed out Lucy. "Then no one will have to interrupt."

"When the sock is completely confused," continued Pandora, ignoring Lucy in her best Miss Watkins fashion, "I want you to hold the biscuit barrel steady. I will cut the tape with Dad's gardening scissors, which you see I have already got out. I will then remove the lid, while at the same time you tip the biscuit barrel into the drawer. The blue sock should flop out next to his soggy friend. With a really good shake I reckon the blue sock should be too dizzy to slink away for at least a couple of minutes. That should give us plenty of time to get the green sock into the drawer.

"The way we'll get the green sock into the drawer is..."

"Before you say anything else, just because you touched the red one I am *not* touching the green one," protested Lucy, jumping rapidly to conclusions. "That's not fair, Pandora, because the green one is by far

124

the nastiest, so touching that one is like touching a hundred red socks. Anyway, you will be using Samson and Delilah's net for the red sock, so that's different, and it will be too wet to open its mouth. Who knows what the green one might do to me with its fangs? There is no way I want a nurse in a plastic pinny to give me an injection against sock disease. You don't know what those injections are like, Pandora. Anyway, if it bites me there might not even be time to get me to the hospital. I could swell up like balloon and explode right here in your dad's shed. Then how will you explain that to my mum, especially with the barbecue? So that's final. I am not going to touch that sock. Just because it's your plan, you can't tell everyone what to do.

"And another thing," Lucy was by now in full flow. "There is no way I am going near Tam's mouth, either. Not after Cedric. What if I accidentally bump into Tam and knock him over? Who knows what he might do to me, Pandora? I don't want to get bitten by a dog and a talking sock in the same day."

"Don't worry, Lucy," reassured Pandora. "Neither of us will actually have to touch the green sock. That's not in my plan. If you'll give me a minute I'll explain."

Pandora pointed to two boxes placed next to the chest of drawers. They were of different sizes and shapes, and together made what appeared to be two steps.

"Tam is going to climb up those boxes with the green sock in his mouth. On my signal, he will shake his head from side to side. This will make the green sock dizzy, too. On my next signal Tam will drop the green sock into the drawer alongside the other two. Tam practiced climbing up and down the boxes while we were waiting for you. So I know that part works. I'm sure he won't have any problems with dropping the sock, either. I've seen Mr. Mower tell Tam to drop his tennis ball lots of times and he always does. After Tam has let go of the green sock we'll quickly lock the drawer with your granny's key."

Lucy looked mightily relieved at Pandora's suggestion. She nodded her head in agreement.

"The socks will be trapped again forever," concluded Pandora. "And we'll never open the drawer again."

"Especially not after we have made our solemn promise," added Lucy.

"Especially not after that," said Pandora. "Though we are only going to adapt the Brownie promise, remember," she added quickly.

"Better make a start, Pandora," said Lucy, catching sight of Pandora's watch. "It's getting really late. I have to get back home soon or Mum will go absolutely crazy."

The girls dealt with the soggy red sock very easily. Pandora hooked it out of the watering can. It was heavier than she had expected and she had to concentrate hard in case it slipped off the end of the tiny fishing net. As she transferred the sock to the drawer huge droplets of water sploshed onto the floor beneath, falling like monsoon rain in the hot and sticky shed. The sock flopped onto the dark wood interior of the open drawer as lifelessly as if it were a mackerel from a stall in the fish market being dropped into a shopping bag. The sock never moved once. From the look on its face it seemed relieved to be out of the water and on a hard surface once more.

The blue sock took considerably more effort. Lucy shook the biscuit barrel for ages. At first the sock shrieked and complained bitterly at being banged about. Eventually the complaints ceased and the sock fell silent. By then Lucy's arms had become both tingly and wobbly, like the long, dangly feelers of an electrified jellyfish. Lucy was immensely grateful when at last she was able to put the biscuit barrel down. Pandora cut through the tape that held the lid secure. Meanwhile Lucy wiggled some life back in her arms and shoulders.

When the feeling had returned sufficiently to her limbs, Lucy lifted the barrel into place beside the drawer. Pandora took hold of the lid and counted to three. On the count of three Pandora pulled off the lid. Lucy tipped the barrel upside down sharply. The blue sock, utterly confused about not just the day of the week but also the month of the year, fell limply into the drawer. It looked as exhausted as an ordinary sock does when it is thrown into the washing basket at the end of a hard day wrapped around a particularly sweaty foot. It lay there as motionless as its partner in crime, though without the same look of relief.

"Only the green sock left, Lucy," said Pandora. Her voice was brimming with satisfaction. The plan was going very well indeed. "Nearly there."

As neither the red nor the blue sock looked as if it was going to stir for a minute or two, and while the green sock was locked tightly in Tam's mouth, Lucy thought it was a good moment to ask a question that had begun to trouble her greatly. It had nagged away like toothache since the socks had first escaped. She had to know the answer before she and Pandora parted for the rest of the day.

"Are you *still* going to keep these socks in your new bedroom, Pandora?" she asked. "I mean, now you know what they can do. When we talked earlier in your kitchen we didn't know what they are really like. Now we do. Are you sure about keeping them locked in the drawer?"

"Yes, Lucy," replied Pandora after the briefest of hesitations. "I am. I want to keep them. At least for a little while."

"But why?" pressed Lucy. "Wouldn't you be better giving them to a wildlife park or something, Pandora? That way they wouldn't cause you any bother. There must be a charity somewhere that looks after talking socks. Granny left some money in her will to a place that looks after retired seaside donkeys and we've had the people from the Owl Sanctuary in school. There are lots of places like that for different things. There must be one for socks."

"That's exactly the point, Lucy," responded Pandora. "I honestly don't think there is such a thing as a Sock Sanctuary, because I don't think there are any other socks anywhere else in the world like these. If there were, then surely Miss Watkins would have told us or we've have heard about it from somewhere. That's why I want to keep them.

"I know keeping them may sound strange after all the trouble they've caused, but I want to find out the answers to some questions. These socks must be unique. I want to know where they come from and how they got to be locked in the drawer. I also want to know how they got to talk and move in the first place. And I want to be the first person in the world to know, Lucy. Once I have the answers, I'll tell everyone what I have discovered. Honestly I will. But until I know, the socks have to stay locked in my room."

"Just think," said Lucy, her eyes widening. "If you do find out those things you'll be a dead famous scientist. Like Charles Darwin or the person who invented oven chips."

"*We'll* be famous," said Pandora generously. "After all, we used your granny's keys. Everyone will know about you, too, Lucy. We'll be partners, like the Montgolfier brothers and their balloon."

"Or the Wright brothers," added Lucy, wanting to show that she had listened during their topic on 'Famous Journeys', too. "Except we'll have to be sisters, though not really. But we could pretend. I know! We could call ourselves, 'The Sock Sisters'."

"We could," said Pandora doubtfully, "But, first, we have to get the green sock inside the drawer. And we can't leave it much longer, Lucy. The other two will start to come round very soon."

Pandora signalled to Tam that it was time for him to do his stuff. He reacted immediately by standing up and wagging his tail. At Pandora's command he scrambled up the boxes. At the top he cocked his head to one side quizzically, awaiting his next instruction.

"Give the sock a really good shake, Tam," ordered Pandora. "Like this." She demonstrated by shaking her head from side to side, gritting her teeth and growling at the same time.

From Tam's response it was as if he had been waiting for this instruction all his life. He shook his head from side to side so enthusiastically that an atomic clock could not have vibrated any faster. So energetic was the shaking that the girls heard even more woollen threads tear apart around the sock's raggedy neck.

"Good boy, Tam," said Pandora, when she was sure the sock would be reeling. Her hands were on the loopy handles of the drawer ready to shut it to. "Put it down now." Pandora jerked her head downwards and opened her mouth to make sure it was obvious what she wanted Tam to do.

Reluctantly, for he was having a truly wonderful time with the sock, Tam turned his head until it was directly over the open drawer. He positioned himself with his head a little to one side, like the bomb aimer of an old aircraft looking down his sights. With a final shake of his head, and one last grizzly snarl at the listless sock, Tam jerked his neck downwards and opened his mouth.

It was as Tam opened his jaws - at the split-second the sock was released and began to free-fall through the air - that it happened. Pandora, Lucy and Tam were caught totally by surprise. None of them saw it coming.

With a sudden and unexpected lunge, like an angry swan thrusting its beak at someone who has strayed too near for comfort, the sock shot its head forward. Its sinister black eyes appeared instantly alive and alert. With its jaws opened wide the sock bit deeply into Pandora's hand. Almost effortlessly, its burning fangs pierced her tender skin like two red-hot needles. The pain was intense. Instinctively, Pandora let go of the drawer. At the same time she jerked her arm into the air as she tried desperately to shake off the sock. Pandora looked for a moment like a swimmer doing the backstroke. The sock, however, would not let go. Its grip on Pandora was unyielding. Pandora's rising hand began to lift the green sock high into the air.

Tam, briefly taken aback by the astonishing spiritedness of the sock, reacted swiftly to what was happening. He leapt from the boxes and dived at the sock. He flew through the air, mouth open. He just managed to catch hold of the end of its tail. If Pandora's hand been a fraction higher Tam would have missed it altogether. With the leg of the sock gripped between his teeth Tam began to fall towards the ground, gravity taking its inevitable course. Pandora's hand, meanwhile, continued to rise.

For an instant, as Tam reached the bottom of his descent and Pandora's hand neared the top of its arc, the now taut sock resembled the shaft of an emerald pendulum. For a brief moment more, like a still photograph, Pandora's hand was halted in mid-air while Tam dangled centimetres above the floor. Between girl and dog the sock was stretched to its uttermost length.

It was inevitable that something would have to give. It was the frayed and torn threads that first conceded defeat. With an awful ripping sound the wool around the heel of the sock began rapidly to tear and unravel.

In no time at all, as the last of the threads snapped apart, Tam plunged to the ground. He landed on the floor of the shed in a heap. In his mouth was the long leg of the sock. It appeared totally lifeless.

The sock's head, however, was still fastened to Pandora's hand, skewered in place by the fangs. At the moment the sock snapped in two, Pandora's arm, which had begun to be pulled downwards, became suddenly free of its counterweight. Her arm began immediately to arc upwards again. Its abrupt release meant that it rose with the force of a Roman catapult loosed from its restraint. As her hand swiftly reached the very top of the arc, the fiery fangs fell away from Pandora's hand. It felt like the jaws of the sock had nothing left to grip with. The force of Pandora's swing propelled the torn remains of the sock out through the open shed door. It soared high over the garden fence and into the distance.

It was all over in seconds.

Lucy, recovering from the shock of the terrible events she had just witnessed, acted promptly. She ordered Tam to get to his feet and scramble up the boxes. Tam obeyed without hesitation. Without ado, he dropped what was left of the green sock into the drawer along with the other two socks. From the way it had come apart Lucy was certain the green sock was dead, but she didn't want to take any chances. Lucy closed the drawer and locked it securely. She then turned to help her injured friend.

Pandora was holding her throbbing hand between her legs. Tears were streaming down her freckled cheeks. They were not simply because of the pain, which was indescribable, but also of frustration at being outwitted once again by the sock. With Lucy's arm around her shoulder Pandora slowly drew out her hand. On her palm and the back of her hand were twin perforations, each a few centimetres apart, from which bubbled tiny droplets of blood. There was no swelling or discolouring near the holes, nothing to indicate that the fangs had deposited any poison. Across the back of Pandora's hand, mirrored on her palm, could be seen the red u-shaped imprint left by the strong grip of the sock's clenching mouth.

"That must really hurt, Pandora," said Lucy tenderly. She examined the injuries carefully. "I think the red marks will go soon, as will the little holes. Looking at them I don't think you'll need an injection. Cedric's bite started to swell up straightaway."

"Where's the sock?" asked Pandora weakly. Her voice had been almost taken away by the shock and speed of what had just occurred.

"Tam put the long bit in the drawer with the other two," replied Lucy. "I've locked the drawer now. The head end shot out of the door as you swung your arm. It went right over the fence. I think it must have landed in Mrs Dunstan's garden. I'll go and pick it up in a minute. It must have died when it snapped apart. That's why it lost its grip."

"Good," sobbed Pandora. "I'm glad it's gone."

"Don't worry. It's as dead as a dodo," said Lucy confidently, though in truth she wasn't terribly sure what a dodo was or even why it was dead.

"You stay here while I take Tam back to Mr. and Mrs Mower's house," she continued. "They will be back soon and we don't want them to find that Tam is missing.

"On the way back round here I'll pick up the rest of that revolting sock. You can tell me later whether you want to sneak it back into the drawer or put it in the dustbin. Then I'll help you to your bedroom. You ought to stay in your room, Pandora, until the marks on your hands have gone down. I'll tell your parents you've got heatstroke from being in the shed and need a sleep. And I'll tell them you don't want to be disturbed. It could be tricky if they start asking questions about the bite marks. Then I'd better get back home to get ready for Auntie Pam's rotten old barbecue."

"Thanks, Lucy," said Pandora. "You're the best friend anyone could ever want."

She paused. "I think I'd better tell my parents the truth, though. I'm not sure I want those socks in my bedroom any more. Not now. They're much too dangerous. This bite has changed my mind."

"We'll tell them, Pandora," said Lucy. "It will be better if we do it together."

Pandora smiled and Lucy grinned in return. Lucy was pleased that Pandora had decided to tell her parents about the socks. Lucy thought that although they would be angry that Pandora hadn't told them, and probably Lucy, too, for that matter, there should be no real problems after that. Once everyone knew that the green sock was dead and the other two were safe everything would be fine. And she and Pandora would still be famous. After all, there were still two talking socks to set before the world. Lucy brightened at the thought. She mused momentarily whether she should change her name to Suzie Sock or Sandra Sock, both of which she thought sounded great, but decided to wait to see what Pandora wanted to call herself before she chose her own name.

Then an even more wonderful thought occurred to her. Once Pandora's parents knew about the socks they were bound to tell all sorts of people about the discovery. Lucy would almost certainly have to give a statement to the police, or perhaps MI5, or even the Prime Minister. Then there would be loads of television interviews. They were bound to take up the rest of the day. All of which would mean she would have to miss Auntie Pam's barbecue! And, best of all, there was absolutely nothing her mum could do about it.

Lucy felt much lighter when she stepped out of the shed with Tam at her side. Even the weather seemed to share Lucy's sudden joy. Beyond the door the garden was filled with glorious summer sunshine. Butterflies trickled through the air like rose petals blown by the wind. Birds chirruped happily in the shelter of the gently shimmering trees. All around was the soothing sound and smell of a balmy afternoon.

"Come on, Tam," said Lucy. "I'll be back in a minute, Pandora. Then we'll tell your mum and dad all about it. I'll bring the other half of that sock back with me as proof."

"See you soon," replied Pandora, nursing her sore hand. "And thanks."

16

In Mrs Dunstan's garden something small and emerald green slithered unnoticed into one of her flowerbeds. A sly smirk settled on its thin black lips as it came to rest beneath a particularly full bush. Its wily eyes, sparkling with success, shone like two round buttons fashioned from the purest ebony.

It could hear the two girls clearly enough. They were talking as if the sock was dead and their troubles all over. The sock scoffed at their stupidity. They knew nothing. In reality their troubles were only just beginning. They would know soon enough when that ridiculous girl finally worked out why the rest of the sock was nowhere to be found.

Slowly, the sock licked its lips with its thin forked tongue. Those girls could not have been more wrong about why it had suddenly withdrawn its fangs. What they had witnessed was, in fact, a perfectly executed escape. Everything had happened exactly according to plan. The sock had fully anticipated their every move, even the dramatic leap of that mangy mongrel. It had been so predictable it had almost taken the fun out of it – but not quite. The sock grinned to itself maliciously.

Then, catching snatches of their conversation, it laughed out loud. The girl was finally going to tell her parents, was she? Presumably, once the pain had lessened, she would regain her composure and, with it, her confidence. He could imagine her telling them how clever she was at capturing the other two and how successful she had been at getting rid of the third sock, even though she couldn't find the torn piece. She was that sort of girl. The sock sneered. Another girl had thought that, too, it remembered, a long, long time ago. And look what happened to her!

It's time to make you truly famous, Pandora, thought the sock, like your namesake. I'll make a start tonight, under cover of darkness. The cat flap will make it so easy to get in and out. Once I'm inside, I'll begin with all those boxes that have been so carefully packed and sealed. Although I won't be able to wait around to hear your feeble excuses, I can well imagine the scene. What a pleasure it will be to spoil things for you! The sock smirked wickedly at the thought.

The sock stopped breathing for a moment. Footsteps were approaching. At their sound the sock pulled itself deeper into the bush. Perfectly camouflaged against the undergrowth the sock watched through the dense foliage as the other girl - the foolish one - came in through the gate and began to nose around. It grinned as, puzzled, she wandered out again after a few minutes. It listened as another gate was opened. It grinned spitefully and hissed to itself, 'Can't find where I am, eh? You'll know later. Or at least you'll know where I've been. Of that you and your best friend will have no doubt'.

The sock thought what it might do after it had paid its respects to Pandora. It could, of course, stay around here. There were lots of possibilities, starting with the silly girl's family, and then the Mowers with their dreadful dog. And it would be such fun to hear Pandora being blamed for all sorts of mischief time and time again. The sock smiled at the delicious thought of messing around in her classroom. What would Miss Watkins think then?

But it fancied new horizons. It had been in the drawer for such a long time. Ever since...well, that was then. Best not to think about it. Best to put the past behind. It certainly didn't intend to be caught like that again. Now was time to begin afresh.

The sock decided it would visit the places it hadn't been to for many, many years. They might have forgotten all about his wickedness and it would be wonderful to remind them! And it hadn't been on one of these new boats, though it knew about them. For weeks it had endured the mindless chatter of the people talking about in its last home, whilst it had been locked away in that keyless drawer. They had been on what they called a cruise and had boasted to their friends and family about it endlessly. The sock had learned these new boats were much bigger and sometimes carried thousands of people. That should give it plenty of sport, all those people to upset and annoy! And it would be easy enough to stow away. If it made its way down to the docks and lay there on the ground looking lost and homeless, like a discarded hand puppet, some ridiculous child making its way aboard would be bound to pick it up and stuff it into a grubby pocket. It was the sort of stupid thing children always did

'Watch out world!' hissed the sock at everyone in general and no one in particular. It felt a surge of energy burst along its threads. I'm back! And it feels SO good.

The sock grinned wickedly once more. It slowly licked the air with its long thin tongue as if tasting all the enjoyment that was to come. Then it settled down, perfectly still, and began waiting for darkness to fall.